W9-BFN-158

Max was waiting for Karinne

Leaning against his car, he eagerly watched the incoming traffic for her. He hadn't seen Karinne enough recently. Between the time she spent working and Max's own schedule, they weren't in physical contact very often. Max missed her so much he ached inside.

Two women climbed out of a just-parked vehicle, but Max only had eyes for Karinne. His pulse quickened at the sight of her. She wore an old pair of denims and a sweatshirt. The childhood blond hair he remembered had long ago deepened to a darker shade, although her green eyes remained the same. Bare toes peeped out from casual summer sandals, and the sweatshirt didn't hide the sweet curves beneath. But his eyes lingered, as always, on her face.

He didn't call out her name. He enjoyed anticipating her beautiful smile of recognition. When she finally caught his gaze, that smile rewarded him.

Dear Reader,

Grand Canyon National Park is famous for its beauty and the river that carved it, the Colorado. The word "canyon," however, is deceptive. Even "Grand" doesn't adequately describe its abundance of life and land mass, its history and ancient culture.

As a child, I grew up walking the Colorado's beds and tributaries high in the Rocky Mountains, searching for gold nuggets. That treasured ore is long gone, but the Colorado River now provides *new* treasure—irrigation and electricity for the Southwest. This means supporting mega-farms, huge crop fields and cities with increasing populations—but modernization has a price.

Sadly, the millennia-old flow into the Gulf of California has disappeared in the past seventy-five years. Long before reaching the sea, the empty riverbed turns to dust. The overconsumption of this now-clear river threatens almost a third of North America's ecosystems, while water and power rights representing billions of dollars are fought in national international courts. The Colorado has replaced the Nile as the most heavily litigated river in the world.

I have taken certain liberties in my story. My description of flooding in the present-day Grand Canyon National Park is now impossible. I have resurrected the "Rogue" Colorado of fifty years ago, before modern technology "tamed" it.

The Hopi believe the Grand Canyon is a *Sipapu*—a sacred place where "The People" emerged to enter the beautiful Southwest. My hero and heroine share this deep respect for the outdoors—and each other. Welcome to the grandest canyon in the world!

And be sure to visit my website, www.paperbackgems.com.

Anne Marie Duquette

The Reluctant Bride

ANNE MARIE DUQUETTE

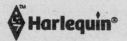

TORONTO NEW YORK LONDON
AMSTERDAM PARIS SYDNEY HAMBURG
STOCKHOLM ATHENS TOKYO MILAN MADRID
PRAGUE WARSAW BUDAPEST AUCKLAND

If you purchased this book without a cover you should be aware that this book is stolen property. It was reported as "unsold and destroyed" to the publisher, and neither the author nor the publisher has received any payment for this "stripped book."

Recycling programs
for this product may
not exist in your area.

ISBN-13: 978-0-373-75352-9

THE RELUCTANT BRIDE

Copyright © 2011 by Anne Marie Duquette

All rights reserved. Except for use in any review, the reproduction or utilization of this work in whole or in part in any form by any electronic, mechanical or other means, now known or hereafter invented, including xerography, photocopying and recording, or in any information storage or retrieval system, is forbidden without the written permission of the publisher, Harlequin Enterprises Limited, 225 Duncan Mill Road, Don Mills, Ontario M3B 3K9, Canada.

This is a work of fiction. Names, characters, places and incidents are either the product of the author's imagination or are used fictitiously, and any resemblance to actual persons, living or dead, business establishments, events or locales is entirely coincidental.

This edition published by arrangement with Harlequin Books S.A.

For questions and comments about the quality of this book please contact us at Customer_eCare@Harlequin.ca

® and TM are trademarks of the publisher. Trademarks indicated with ® are registered in the United States Patent and Trademark Office, the Canadian Trade Marks Office and in other countries.

www.eHarlequin.com

Printed in U.S.A.

ABOUT THE AUTHOR

Anne Marie enjoys the Southern California lifestyle with her husband, two grown children and two grandchildren. When she's not reading or writing, she's relaxing on the beach—or upping her adrenaline on Disneyland's roller coasters. Her stories focus on the security *and* the adventure of romance because she feels every relationship should have both!

Don't miss any of our special offers. Write to us at the following address for information on our newest releases.

Harlequin Reader Service
U.S.: 3010 Walden Ave., P.O. Box 1325, Buffalo, NY 14269
Canadian: P.O. Box 609, Fort Erie, Ont. L2A 5X3

My most heartfelt gratitude to Paula E.,
editor, teacher and friend.
Thank you for everything!

Max had called, as promised. If Karinne could sho

Chapter One

Her mother couldn't be alive...could she?

In ordinary circumstances, Karinne Cavanaugh should be smiling as she packed for vacation. The Grand Canyon, one of the most spectacular parks in the world, awaited her photographer's eye. For once she wouldn't be photographing men in sports uniforms. She'd be lost in the blissful glory of the Southwest's July landscape. As an added bonus, she'd get to see her fiancé, Max Hunter. Their wedding would be in the fall at the Grand Old Lodge—seventy-five years old—three times her age, and boasting many other weddings in the past. She was driving up to Flagstaff to actually see the place for herself.

Max, a rafting guide, had even promised a longer raft trip instead of their short weekend treks down the Colorado River at Karinne's urging—a prehoneymoon vacation.

"Since we're getting married, I should be more familiar with what you do for a living," she'd coaxed him with a kiss. "It'll be romantic."

"I wish you'd said something sooner. I'm already booked, Karinne," Max warned, although he didn't resist her kisses. Rafting trips were booked years in advance, rain or shine. "But if I get a cancellation, I'll call you."

A cancellation *had* occurred during rainy weather, and Max had called, as promised. If Karinne could show up

in two days, she'd be in luck. Max worked a single craft
in the rafting concession with his younger brother, Cory.
The brothers had outfitted a private expedition that had
canceled, despite the deposit. Her own boss agreed to the
short notice. She and Max could check out the wedding and
honeymoon accommodations sooner rather than later. The
trip down the river would be just the two of them, a few precious days together before their wedding in November. She
should consider herself the luckiest woman in the world.

Karinne Cavanaugh, engaged, educated and employed,
didn't know what to think.

Her mother, long thought dead, a woman who'd disappeared during Karinne's childhood, had seemingly come
back to haunt her.

During one of Karinne's home-game baseball photography sessions, she'd caught a familiar face in the background
crowd. This in itself was rare. She clicked off some rapid
shots. Seconds later, the woman was gone; whoever the
"double" was didn't return.

On her computer afterward, Karinne ignored her work
photos, digitally enlarging the crowd pictures first. They
showed a woman who could very well be an older Margot
Cavanaugh—except that Margot hadn't been seen in more
than twenty years. She'd parked at the side of an Arizona
river, left a suicide note in her car and disappeared.

There hadn't been a body to bury; recovery efforts had
been unproductive. That very afternoon a seasonal monsoon storm of epic proportions had struck with enough
precipitation to cause whitecaps on the overflowing Arizona irrigation canals for two full days. Even rescue and
recovery personnel couldn't cover much ground. People
died every year during the flash floods, on foot, in cars
and the arroyo washes.

Jeff Cavanaugh's mother, a widow, had moved in to take

care of her grieving son and granddaughter. Karinne's care-free days of childhood were over.

Karinne grew up next door to the Hunters. Max, the older boy, had been her lifeline. Karinne's parents had hardly ever been home together and, when they were, fought bitterly over whose photographic career and next assignment was more important. Their marriage problems had often driven her to the Hunters' home. But after her mother's death, an eerie stillness had replaced the bitter fights at home. Karinne found herself at the Hunters' more than ever.

Karinne's father cut back on his work hours, and her grandmother stayed until Karinne's senior year of high school before moving to Florida. Karinne inherited her mother's cameras and flair for photography. She'd graduated, gone to college and now had a job she enjoyed. Plus, the boy next door, Max Hunter, loved her as much as she loved him. Nothing could burst Karinne's joy....

Until that apparent double had showed up at the baseball game just a few weeks ago. Karinne hadn't told her father, although she'd checked with the police and filed a report. The intake officer had taken the disk with the digital copies, nodded and merely said he'd "keep them on file." A plainclothes detective in the same office had been kinder. She'd scanned the last photo the family had of Margot and plugged it into the computer simulation software to "age" the image. She'd even agreed there was a likeness.

"I'll make sure this gets into our computers," the detective said. "But your mother's disappearance was ruled a suicide drowning. I wouldn't hold out any hope, Ms. Cavanaugh."

"They never found her body. Could you recommend a private detective?" Karinne had asked.

"We can't, and even if we could, I wouldn't recommend it."

Karinne racked her brain. "I understand the Red Cross is very good at finding missing people. Like those lost in earthquakes or hurricanes."

"Yes, but we're talking about recent victims, Ms. Cavanaugh. I know it's hard for family to give up hope, but it's been years. If it were me," the detective had added softly, "I'd let it end right here."

Karinne tried. Once home, she'd put the disk with the enlargements in her filing cabinet. She'd withdrawn the neatly folded aged photo printout from her purse and tossed it in the trash. But later she dug it out and carefully filed it away. The next day she'd gone to a private detective, who gave her the same advice as the police. He also refused to take the case or her money, and warned her about others who might not be as scrupulous.

Karinne prayed she was overreacting. She decided to let matters rest—until last week. Her father, somewhat obsessed with mortality in his older years, had asked how Karinne would feel if he ever sold the house. The question had shocked her and she'd stuttered, "But th-then...Mom couldn't f-find us."

Her father's surprised reaction and "Karinne, what's wrong?" prompted her to come clean with him.

"Dad, I'm just not sure what to think," Karinne said. Reluctantly, feeling somewhat foolish, she showed her father the digital photos, the "aged" picture and the police report she'd filed. To her relief, her father looked and listened; he didn't laugh. On the old couch, they sat side by side, his arm around her shoulders.

"There is some resemblance," he agreed. "But your photos aren't that clear, and your mother's dead. I wish you'd come to me earlier."

"I sound crazy, don't I?"

"No, sweetheart. You sound perfectly normal. You're

an engaged woman who simply wishes her mother could be at her wedding."

"You think that's all it is?"

"Yes." Jeff stroked his daughter's blond hair. "I've been having the same thoughts myself. How Margot would've loved shopping for a dress with you. How she'd smile when we walked down the aisle. She loved you so much." His own eyes grew moist, and he gestured at the printouts in her lap. "Don't let these ruin your wedding, Karinne. You've already postponed it twice because of my health. You and Max have a great future. Your mother will be there in spirit to bless your union."

"Thanks, Dad." Karinne and her father hugged, and that had been the end of it—until yesterday, when a package had arrived, the day before she was to leave for the rafting trip. Inside was a hooded pink sweatshirt bearing the words Grand Canyon Village across the front. She assumed the package was from her fiancé.

"Max…" She smiled and looked for a note with his bold handwriting. She shook out the sweatshirt, and a typed note fluttered out, but it wasn't from Max.

"I want to see you. If you feel the same, wear this on your trip. Love, Mom."

ALTHOUGH NOT a superstitious woman, Karinne wondered if the goose bumps on her arms meant serious trouble ahead. If she hadn't wanted to check out the wedding and reception location, she would've considered canceling her trip. But that seemed cowardly, and then she'd have to tell Max why. What should she do?

The sweatshirt still lay stuffed inside her dresser drawer. She hadn't gone back to the police or told anyone about it. There wasn't much to tell from an evidence point of view. The mailing address was on a label from the canyon's gift store; it wasn't hand-printed. There was no return address on the note. Someone was either playing a very sick joke or trying to ruin her peace of mind.

Karinne gave up on neatly arranging her underwear and shoved a handful of panties into the backpack she needed for her trip. The sooner she saw Max, the better she'd feel.

There was a knock at her bedroom door. Her roommate, Anita, Cory's wife, peeked in when Karinne responded.

With Cory working in northern Arizona and Anita working in central Arizona, the apartment was a weekday home for Anita. She spent weekends at the Grand Canyon with her husband. They'd been married only a year, and Anita had chosen to keep her current job until they could save enough to buy their own home up north.

Karinne envied her friend. She usually spent weekends working sporting events and wasn't happy with her limited time with Max. After all, they'd been engaged for two long years, yet rarely saw each other. Somehow their wedding kept getting pushed back.... She'd changed the date three times.

"You're home early. You take a half day off?" Karinne immediately asked.

Anita eyed her backpack. "Packing for your minivacation?" The expression on Anita's normally cheerful face was drawn.

"I leave tomorrow. What's up?"

"I got fired."

"Fired?" Karinne echoed.

"Yes. Can you believe it?"

Karinne shoved aside her backpack, leaving room on the bed for Anita to sit. "What happened? No one in their right mind would fire you."

"They might as well have. Technically, I got laid off. So

did a bunch of others. It could be for months...or for good."
She flopped onto the bed next to Karinne. "I can't believe
it! I mean, management gave us warning, but I've been
there for five years. The things is, the company's losing
money."

"Oh, no..."

"Oh, yeah." Anita worked for a local commuter airline.
She'd graduated from college with a degree in accounting
and had landed a plum job in the finance department right
away, quite an accomplishment for someone with no experience. She'd kept that job after marrying Cory Hunter.
Unfortunately, many airlines had suffered serious financial
difficulties in light of increased costs and the latest national
recession. Several had declared bankruptcy; layoffs had
been the norm rather than the exception at Anita's corporate
office.

"I'm so sorry," Karinne said.

"Maybe you can find me something," Anita said mourn-
fully. "At least you're safe. Talk about job security. No one
ever downsizes in professional sports."

Karinne's job as sports photographer for a consortium
was quite secure. Even during recessions, professional
baseball and football never lost favor with the public. The
Diamondbacks and the Cardinals were her specialty. She'd
always been a devoted techie when it came to computers,
and her skill as a digital photographer had quickly garnered
attention.

The Cavanaugh name was well-known. Despite her
youth and the tradition of male photographers in men's
locker rooms, at the team owners' personal request, Karinne handled much of the workload. Everyone knew her
qualifications and could vouch for her get-along-with-
everyone character. She concentrated on capturing digital
stills of professional athletes in motion, stills that could be

sent instantly to media news sources on the internet and posted just as quickly.

"What am I gonna do?" Anita moaned. "I'm unemployed!"

"Something will come up," Karinne assured her.

"When? It won't be easy to get a job as good as my old one. I had great benefits, too."

"Nita, I'm so sorry," Karinne said again.

Anita stared at the open backpack. "I'm surprised you're taking time off. Baseball season isn't over."

"I'm a bride on a mission. My boss knows it, and I've got plenty of vacation hours on the books. I can use it or lose it." Karinne gestured to the backpack. "I'm definitely using it. Max had a cancellation on a rafting trip."

"If you two weren't such lovebirds, I'd ask if I could I come along, too. I've certainly got the time now," Anita said, her voice rueful.

Karinne hesitated, not wanting to be rude or to hurt her friend's feelings. Max and Karinne were rarely together, and she missed him terribly. Their last reunion had been months ago.

Cory and Karinne had attended school together from first grade on. Both of their families still owned the same homes on the same street. Anita and Karinne, on the other hand, met as computer-assigned college roommates. The computer had glitched; Anita had wanted a friend from high school as her roommate, while Karinne had requested a single room. Anita had originally planned to refuse the dorm room, but the two women hit it off instantly. As an added bonus, Anita had met Cory. The two married, despite the warnings of family and friends that a long-distance marriage was gambling with the future.

Karinne worried about that, too. Would her own marriage be at risk? Her parents had both traveled extensively, and it sure hadn't helped.

The wedding was only a few months away. Max's job rafting down the Colorado River in the Grand Canyon made casual get-togethers geographically difficult, if not impossible, while her job as sports photographer meant she accompanied the teams on out-of-state games.

"If you don't mind giving me a ride, we could split up when we get there. I could stay with Cory at the guys' place," Anita suggested. "Maybe I can do some wedding legwork for you."

"Of course you're welcome to ride up with me. And to come rafting, if you want. But you've never seemed interested in the water," Karinne said slowly, her desire to be alone with Max warring with sympathy for her roommate.

"I'm interested in anything that would cheer me up. I can foot the bill," Anita insisted.

"I'm not concerned. You know that."

"I didn't get a chance to tell you," Anita added. "But Cory said if you don't mind, four would be better than two for the raft trip."

"When did you talk to him?" Karinne asked, confused.

"A few days ago. I was working at the time, so I said no. He just called me again today, though. They have extra provisions because of the cancellation, and he doesn't want to waste the perishables."

"Oh." Karinne blinked.

"If you'd rather I didn't come," Anita backtracked, "I'll stay topside with Cory and update my résumé. Review the want ads. Do some wedding preparations for you."

Karinne hated seeing Anita's disappointment. So far this vacation had been full of surprises, and it hadn't even started yet. She thought of the pink sweatshirt still in her drawer, and the goose bumps ran down her neck again. If a ghost intended to show up, maybe having reinforcements around wasn't such a bad idea. And if Cory had invited his wife rafting, it wasn't Karinne's place to tell them no.

"Forget the want ads. There's plenty of time for that later." Karinne gestured with her chin. "Get packing. We'll start the drive north early tomorrow morning."

Chapter Two

The rain continued its steady downfall. Arizona forecasters didn't call it the monsoon season for nothing. Moisture-laden air from the Pacific's California coast hit the Rocky Mountains and rose high to cross the peaks. The moisture moved toward the hotter air above the desert, where its coolness clashed with the heat, mushrooming in purple thunderheads that drenched the area in violent downpours with stick, chain and ball lightning.

Inside the personal quarters provided for park concessionaires topside, Max Hunter stared out the window, fascinated as always by the force of water. Harnessed correctly, it could water the desert and quench the thirst of millions of plants, animals and humans. Left to its elemental nature, water would erode the canyon below, just as it had in prehistoric times.

The Colorado—Spanish for red—was one of the nation's three ancient, prehistoric rivers, along with Utah's Green River and the Mississippi. The Colorado continued carving the massive canyons with its abrasive red silt, fed by the rain and snowfall of the Rocky Mountains.

"Tourists want sunshine. If this keeps up, they'll have

to open the spill gates upriver, then who knows what the white-water conditions will be this weekend. We'll have to do more of the trip on foot," Cory grumbled.

"If it wasn't for the weather, we couldn't have invited Karinne and Anita up," Max reminded him. "Although I thought it would just be me and Karinne," he said with a trace of annoyance. A long-distance courtship, preface to what would be a long-distance marriage, made Max cherish whatever time he could spend with his fiancée, especially time alone. Unfortunately, Cory suffered from the same problem. But at least Cory had made faster progress. He'd become engaged, gotten married and was saving for a house with his wife, even though Max and Karinne had been engaged first. Karinne had been dragging her feet, and Max was tired of it. He'd hoped that this long trek down the river would settle things once and for all. Yes, their wedding was planned for November, but it wouldn't be the first time Karinne had put it off. If it wasn't her father's health, it was her job demands. The timing never seemed to be right for her.

Cory sensed Max's irritation.

"I figured we might as well use up the perishable food, but I told you, I can hang with Anita topside if you want," he said.

"No, that would be rude, and besides, you're right. We're already provisioned for a larger party."

Max added a few more morose comments about foolish tourists who thought deserts were all cacti and sunshine. But his comments reflected his frustration at having a long-distance fiancée. While Cory tuned his guitar, Max remained at the window, which took in the canyon rim wooded area, log-style smaller cabins and lodge.

Although both brothers were deeply tanned and healthy from outdoor work, there the resemblance ended. Blond and blue-eyed like his father, a cruise-ship captain, Cory looked more like a California surfer. He wore his hair fairly long, and sported the attitude of what he was at heart—a musician who was happy anywhere, provided he had his woman and his guitar at his side.

"At least you two will share the same tent for a few days," Cory said to Max. He shook his head. "Although how you two expect to have a marriage, let alone kids, while you're living in opposite ends of the state is beyond me. Karinne doesn't want to quit her job, and you can't. There's no way just one person can run the raft expeditions. Plus there's Jeff's *bad heart* to consider."

"We'll manage. You and Anita have."

"Anita and I are in no hurry for children. You and Karinne are."

"I used to think Karinne wanted children right away," he said morosely. "She said she wanted her dad to see his grandchildren before he died. But talk isn't action. At this rate I'll be old and gray before we ever get to the altar. And Jeff will be long gone."

"Would you still marry her if she changed her mind? Didn't want a family?"

"I don't know."

Cory wisely said nothing, and let Max continue to stare out the window.

Even as a child, Max found inner peace in the unique ruggedness of northern Arizona, although there'd been a time when he'd hated the rawness of the land. That time had come after Margot Cavanaugh's disappearance into the desert.

Margot had showed up at Max's house on that last day, looking for Karinne. Margot's manner had been decidedly off-key, and because of that Max had—uncharacteristically—lied. He remembered the incident clearly, even though he'd been only ten years old.

"No, I don't know where Karinne is, Mrs. C," he'd fibbed, although Karinne and Cory were in his bedroom playing video games. It was Cory's favorite pastime, although six-year-old Karinne wasn't as skilled.

"Are you sure?" Margot pressed. "She told me she was coming here."

The hair on the back of the boy's neck rose as Margot grabbed his arm.

"She left." Max pulled his arm away from Margot, who quickly stepped back and hurried off the porch. Max carefully dead-bolted the door before rubbing at his arm. Something about Margot's strange mood and aggressive behavior unnerved him and came back to haunt him when Margot's suicide note was discovered.

Later, Max didn't regret his decision. At least Margot's death was a single tragedy, not a double one involving Karinne's death, too. Max had never spoken of it to anyone except Cory. He thanked the gods of chance that he'd answered the door that fateful day, and Karinne had survived her mother's disappearance.

"I don't know how you expect to have kids when neither of you wants to quit your job," Cory said, thumbing his guitar strings. "You won't be able to raise them together. In fact, you won't be able to raise them at all."

Max refused to rise to the bait. "We're not even married yet, Cory."

"And you won't stay married long if you don't get serious about your situation. You can't bring infants and baby bottles into white-water rafts, and Karinne can't bring children to her sporting events. You've had the longest engagement on record, and you're still hiding your heads in the sand. One of you has to quit, Max."

"She'll probably stay home with them once they're born."

"Have you guys even talked about this? Maybe she doesn't want to choose children over her career. Your marriage will be off to a rocky start if you don't get this settled."

That remark drew Max away from the window. "Thanks a lot. We haven't even had the wedding, and you've already got us divorced."

"Not me," said Cory. "You and Karinne. She's still looking after her father, and you're still waiting for Karinne's mother to turn up and ruin everything."

"They never found her body," Max slowly said. "And Margot wanted a divorce. She and Jeff were always fighting. That suicide note could've been a fake. She could've taken the opportunity to run. I remember her well, Cory. She wasn't interested in being a wife and mother. And there were whispers about her having a gambling problem."

Cory sighed. "So let's say Margot *does* come back. So what? You have nothing to fear."

"Come on, we were both home with Karinne the day Margot disappeared. I lied and said I didn't know where she was. If Margot ever returns, what am I going to tell Karinne?"

"Tell her the same thing you told Jeff and the police when they came looking for Margot. That Mom was next door at the neighbors, Dad was at work, you saw Margot, and you did what you thought was right at the time. I don't know why you didn't tell her this years ago."

"Jeff asked me not to because he thought it would be too traumatic. But I may have to after all."

"Why?" Cory asked.

Max paused, then admitted, "I've been getting anonymous phone calls. It's happened three times. Once the caller actually said she was Margot Cavanaugh and asked me for money to come and see Karinne."

"Hell!"

"I went to the police, but nothing. I haven't received any more calls since the last one, so the police weren't able to trace her."

"No wonder you're talking in your sleep."

Max winced. "Not again."

"Yes. You talk about that day Margot came to the door, Max. One of these days, Karinne's gonna hear you."

Icy chills shivered down Max's back. "What do I say?"

"The same thing you always used to say. *Don't tell Karinne.*"

Chapter Three

"At least it's dry for now," Karinne said behind the steering wheel. The freeway had dried off enough for the high-speed driving no longer possible in more populated areas.

Anita turned off the weather station on the car's radio. The day before, they'd left Phoenix before sunrise, and driven one hundred and forty-five miles to Flagstaff. Last night they'd checked into a hotel and were up early again this morning to finish the distance between Flagstaff and Grand Canyon Village. They'd meet the Hunter brothers in less than an hour. Although the skies were cloudy and gray, the deluge had ended last night, and the women were making good time.

"The sun should come out this afternoon," Anita said. She reached for her take-out cup of coffee.

"Fingers crossed," Karinne said. "Or we'll have a wet hike all the way down to the river."

"It's only a day hike," Anita said cheerfully. "A mile straight down."

"Fifteen trail miles, and it's monsoon season, remember? We're gonna get wet."

"I know," Anita said. "But it can't rain the whole time. I

want to take pictures. I brought along a waterproof digital camera."

Karinne smiled. "Maybe you can let me pay for copies, then."

"You didn't bring a camera?"

"Lord, no. I need a break. I'm tired of looking at view screens and through lenses."

"It's driving you crazy?" Anita asked sympathetically.

Karinne thought of her last batch of photos showing the woman who reminded her of her mother.

"You have no idea," she said wryly. "Besides, this way I can spend more time with Max." Karinne had always loved him. Her memories of Max went so far back she couldn't tell when childhood worship and friendship had changed into adult love and passion.

"It'll be good to see Max again," Anita said. "He leaves the canyon area about as often as Cory does."

"Which isn't often."

"My family wishes I'd married someone local, but I can't imagine being with anyone but Cory," Anita said.

"Well, the upside of losing your job is that now you'll have plenty of time to spend with him."

Anita nodded. "I'm tired of us being apart. Maybe I can find new employment up north. Married people shouldn't be separated for such long periods."

Karinne said nothing. She'd often thought the same thing, as had Max. But Max couldn't quit his job, and she didn't want to quit hers. Besides, Jeff Cavanaugh had heart problems and had no other family around, so she felt obliged to stay close to him. Both Karinne and his doctor knew Jeff didn't take his medication regularly. Whether it was due to forgetfulness or a deliberate attempt to keep his daughter's attention, the result was the same.

"Hey, where's your ring?" Anita asked curiously.

"My diamond? At home. I felt it would be safer." At the last minute, Karinne had removed it—and packed the pink sweatshirt.

"It seems strange to see you without it. In fact, with your jobs, I don't know how you two ever got engaged. Good thing you were childhood sweethearts."

Karinne frowned at the old-fashioned term. "Not really." Her love for Max was based on deep trust since childhood, not some clichéd idea like that.

"How would you describe it, then?" Anita teased.

"Call it destiny, and leave it at that," Karinne said lightly. "Max and I grew into each other. He's the man for me." Karinne darted a quick glance at her friend. "But we all can't be as lucky as you and Cory, the perfect couple. Even miles apart, you're happy."

"We're not perfect," Anita said. "And I *am* happy. But I'd be happier if I could be with him *all* the time."

"So would I. With Max, I mean." She and Max were at a stalemate about the subject of one of them relocating. Karinne appreciated that Max loved his job, but so did she. Not only that, Jeff was too ill to be moved, or, at least, claimed he was.

She remembered their argument the last time she'd postponed the wedding.

"You're using your father as an excuse, Karinne. With his heart, he should be in an assisted-care facility. Your living at home is no substitute for professional care."

"He'd be miserable at some nursing home!"

"He'd have a fuller, healthier life than he does right now. We can move him up near us if you want. And no—" he held up a hand when she would have protested "—he isn't too ill to be moved. He just says that because he doesn't want to leave his home. But it's time, and his doctor agrees," Max insisted.

"How would you like giving up your home?" Karinne countered.

"If I had to, I hope I would do it gracefully. But that's not the issue. You know how hard Cory and I have worked to make our concession a success. Do you want me to give it up when I've finally become profitable? And ruin Cory's finances in the process?"

"No, but—"

"I'm not trying to be heartless, Karinne. But Cory and I still have to make a living. Support our families, if we have any. You were the one who wanted Jeff to see his grandchildren," he reminded her.

Karinne flushed. "I know."

That last argument had convinced her to take the week off and spend more time with Max. Their weekends were usually filled with loving reunions in bed, and lately talking seemed to make things worse. Now Anita and Cory were coming along—but it was Cory's business, too.

"Well, all four of us will be together this weekend," Anita continued. "I'm glad you don't mind me tagging along. If you need privacy, just let us know. Maybe we can split up into pairs. I can catch a mule down with Cory," Anita suggested. "I've never ridden a mule."

"Mules are usually booked six months in advance. Unless you grow wings, we're all hiking." Karinne's well-worn hiking boots were in the car trunk.

"Cupid's wings are the only wings we'll be seeing," Anita teased. "What with your wedding and all." She paused. "I wonder why your father hasn't remarried after all this time."

"Dad can't get remarried! He's..." Widowed? *Still married?*

"What?" Anita asked.

"Too old," she quickly substituted.

"I didn't think you'd mind if he did."

"If the circumstances were right, I wouldn't," Karinne replied. "Let's please get through one wedding at a time, okay?"

"You shouldn't make it sound like a chore. This is your future we're talking about."

Karinne exhaled. "You're right. I'm nervous, that's all."

"Let *me* be the nervous one. I just got fired and I have to find a new job. Wish me luck."

"Good luck," Karinne said sincerely, trying hard to hide her envy.

I can't believe it. I'm jeulous of Anita—even though she lost her job. She gets to be with her husband.

"You really mean it?" Anita asked. "You might be losing a roommate."

Karinne nodded. "Of course."

"Wouldn't it be great if you could work in the Grand Canyon area yourself?"

"There aren't any jobs for sports photographers and I don't want to freelance doing nature pictures. Too much competition and not enough money. There's no sense wishing for the impossible."

Even if she wanted things to be different.

Grand Canyon Village parking area

LEANING AGAINST his car, Max eagerly watched the incoming traffic for Karinne. He and Cory had taken a single vehicle to meet the women. Lodging vacancies were scarce and traffic was heavy, despite the overcast sky and "sometimes-yes, sometimes-no" sun. The Grand Canyon was open all year, and according to the visitor count, one of the most popular vacation destinations in the world. Thousands swarmed to see one of nature's true great wonders. The temperatures inside the canyon desert were warm year-round, even when desert tundra winter cold enveloped the land at rim level. But summertime in Arizona was peak season for tourists and locals alike to experience the rainbow of colors the Colorado River had etched through rocks a mile high. The South Rim parking lots overflowed with trolling cars and frustrated drivers. The Hunter brothers fortunately had employee parking passes.

"I want to visit with Karinne, too," Cory reminded his brother. "Try not to hog her too much."

"Can't promise anything," Max said with a grin. "Besides, I expect you and Anita to be holed up in your tents getting reacquainted. Like Karinne and I will."

"That should be them," Cory said.

"Where?" Max asked, excited about seeing his lover and fiancée for the first time in months.

Cory jerked his chin toward the arrivals area. Two women climbed out of a parked vehicle, but Max only had eyes for Karinne. He'd recognize her anywhere, and his pulse quickened at the sight. She traveled light—no camera slung over her shoulder—and was clad in a worn pair of denims and her gray sweatshirt. The blond hair he remembered from childhood had long ago deepened to a darker blond, although her green eyes remained the same. Bare toes peeped out from casual summer sandals, and the sweatshirt didn't hide the curves beneath. But his eyes lingered on her face.

He didn't call out her name. He enjoyed anticipating her beautiful smile of recognition. When she finally caught his gaze, that smile always rewarded him.

"Max!" Karinne shouted. The four gathered together. Max hugged Karinne, loving the feel of her against his body. Then Karinne hugged Cory.

"Isn't this *great?*" Karinne said. "The four of us together again."

Cory kissed Anita on the mouth, then both cheeks. Glossy black hair around a bronze face with dark eyes and high cheekbones reminded Max of Spanish nobility in the early days of Mexico. Anita was exquisitely beautiful. Max appreciated beauty and was the first to acknowledge it—but his sister-in-law had never tickled his hormones like Karinne.

"Karinne, why don't you ride with me in the Jeep? Cory, you and Anita can follow, okay?"

Max hugged Karinne's shoulders with one arm as the other pair split off. They sauntered toward his vehicle, and got in.

"How was your drive up?" Max asked, his hand resting on her thigh, her fingers entwined with his.

"Too long and too wet. I'm glad I'm here." She squeezed his fingers.

"So am I." Max stopped at the intersection light. He took the opportunity to kiss her before the light turned green.

"I've missed you," he said, watching the traffic as he gradually accelerated. "How's your father?"

"Fine."

"And you?"

"Okay."

"Sounds like something's *not* okay." He always knew when Karinne was troubled. He had when they were children, and still did. "What's up?"

"I thought it was strange that Cory invited Anita rafting," Karinne replied. "I thought this trip was supposed to be just for us."

Max shrugged. "He wanted to save on the food stuff. We can only freeze so much of it. But the main reason is that he misses her."

"Well, she has plenty of time to visit now," Karinne said. "Anita just lost her job."

"Yeah, Cory told me." Max stopped at a four-way stop sign. "I'm sorry to hear it."

"Anita wants to get a job up here. Wish I could." Karinne sighed.

"I just thought you'd be tired of sports by now."

"Hey, I was the girl's softball champ, remember? I love sports." Karinne adjusted her sunglasses.

"Don't you get tired of traveling?"

"Sometimes."

"That won't change after we're married, either... Not with me living here and you working in Phoenix. You could always switch to landscapes—plenty of scenery."

"Dad's older and he isn't well. He can't really move. And when it comes to postcard and calendar shots, they don't pay enough. Still, I'd love to be able to earn a living with material like this." Karinne gestured at her open window. The wooded area of northern Arizona and the Coconino Forest shone a brilliant green from the night's rain. It was the "earn a living" part that posed a problem.

"Can't blame you there." Max pointed to the left.

A doe and her fawn browsed the tender young leaves on a shrub, unconcerned with habitual park traffic. Karinne followed the pair with her eyes until the Jeep's path around a winding curve put the deer out of sight.

"It sure beats a sweaty athlete with a bat or ball in his hands," Max said.

"Well, maybe if *you're* the model," Karinne hedged. Cute shots of fawns in the forest were a dime a dozen. Her action shots with professional athletes were unique. "One of these days you'll pose for me, Max."

"In a suit at our wedding," he told her.

"What about during our honeymoon?"

"Just scenery stuff. No jock shots," he insisted. Her wicked smile at his unintentional pun prompted Max to add, "You know what I mean."

"I have other plans for our honeymoon," she promised.

"Have you talked to your dad about those assisted living homes?"

Karinne bit her lip. "I—uh—haven't got to that yet."

"Checking out the homes or telling Jeff it's what his doctor recommends?"

"Neither," she said with a sigh.

"I'm surprised you even agreed to come up for the week, you're so busy protecting your father."

"Please, Max, let's not argue. I just got here."

"We have some things to discuss this week, Karinne. Either we settle them, or…"

"Or what?" Karinne asked. "You're giving me an ultimatum?"

"At least I'm willing to give something new a try for the sake of our relationship. Which is more than you'll do. You're going to argue, aren't you?"

Karinne sighed again and turned her head away. He could rarely say no to her. Maybe that was his problem. Max relented.

"You and Anita have breakfast? Did you bring boots? Hats?"

Karinne nodded. "We ate. And we have everything ready for the hike down."

"How about a mule ride?"

"But…I thought they were booked."

"The park service had two cancellations. They said we could have the slots if we'd piggyback their mule-pack gear down with our regular chopper load supplies," Max said, referring to the chopper delivery service the concessions often used. "One couple can ride, the other can fly. Your choice."

Karinne nodded. "Anita would love the flight. I'd rather savor the quiet. And you."

"We might lose the sun again," Max warned, smiling at her response.

"That's not a very romantic answer," Karinne replied.

"I'm saving the romance for after tonight, since we'll be in a dorm. Sorry, but all we're allowed is a good-night kiss."

"I can drag that out for quite a while," she said merrily.

"Ms. Cavanaugh, you're a woman after my own heart."

Chapter Four

Bright Angel Trailhead,
South Rim, Grand Canyon

The sun finally broke through the clouds as the four re-grouped in the parking area outside the small airport that served the Grand Canyon.

"Are you *positive* you don't want to take the helicopter?" Anita tried to hide her eagerness.

"I've been. You go," Karinne replied. "This will be your first time, won't it?" she asked, already knowing the answer.

"Yes. Thanks, I can't wait." Anita grinned.

"Guess Anita and I will meet you down below," Cory said.

"You want my help loading the supplies?" Max asked.

"I can handle it. You two get your mules," Cory said.

"Enjoy your flight," Karinne told them.

"We'll see you this evening," Max added.

Karinne tilted back her head, shading her eyes as the prop wash of the helicopter blew over their heads. Anita and Cory's journey would be far faster than hers, but she didn't mind. She and Max stood apart from the crowd of tourists waiting for the trip down.

"You nonriders don't need to worry," the park's head

mule wrangler explained to the group standing outside the corral. "These mules could make the trip blindfolded. Just sit back for the ride and let them do their job. The drop-off side of the trail might seem close, but don't let that scare you. We've never lost a mule or rider yet. Listen up as I call out your name and assign you a mount."

Karinne listened, one hand holding the upper pipe bar of the corral, the other still shading her eyes as she stared across the majesty of the Grand Canyon. Nowhere else did reds, pinks, oranges, browns and royal purples blend into such a rich tapestry of bands. Within the canyon, towering spires of layered colors descended one mile down into the Colorado River. Even though she'd seen it before, memory couldn't do justice to the reality of its grandeur. The huge size of the canyon, two hundred and seventeen miles long and from four to eighteen miles wide, provided a huge canvas for nature's most famous colors. Most canyons were dark holes, with scattered green vegetation to break up the browns. Not this one—it was a brilliant rainbow that glistened from top to bottom and side to side.

Karinne listened as the park ranger went into more safety details; the mules took the same trail day after day, year after year, making them safe for nonriders and children.

"Does Cory still ride?" Karinne whispered. She and Cory had learned together one summer.

Max shook his head. "No. The day he got his driver's license was the day he quit using a saddle."

"That's too bad," Karinne said. "He was always good with animals."

As an only child, Karinne had riding lessons, ballet lessons, singing lessons and had participated in scouting. Karinne's lack of pitch made music lessons difficult, and she'd quit scouting when her best friend, Cory, couldn't come camping with "the girls." And although a graceful child, she'd found dance boring. However, the riding lessons for her and Cory had been a huge success, even though her present lifestyle—and extensive traveling—prevented her from indulging in a pastime she still enjoyed.

The head wrangler continued his talk as Max asked, "You've never ridden mules, have you?"

"No, but I guess the principle's the same, isn't it?"

"The gait's a bit different. And since they're sterile, they're more docile."

Karinne knew mules were the product of a male donkey and a female horse. Owners claimed mules were more intelligent than either donkeys or horses. Even the ancient Romans and Greeks had bred and valued them for transport, while Old Mexico preferred mules to horses for cavalry soldiers.

"Mules can see all four feet. Horses can't. That's why the early miners used them," Max explained.

"I just thought the mules would be…larger. These seem…small."

"Not that small," Max contradicted, "but the park mules are deliberately bred from the smaller quarter-horse mares. Anything larger wouldn't be able to handle the narrowness of the trail," he said.

Just then, the second park ranger, a woman, asked, "Anyone here afraid of heights?"

Karinne and Max ignored the wranglers' sharp appraisal of the crowd. She'd never been afraid of heights or horses. She doubted she'd be afraid on a mule.

"If you are, now's the time to admit it. There's no shame in being honest, people, and no place for rider panic attacks. There's only one stopping point on the way down—the Tonto formation," the male ranger said.

There was some murmuring in the crowd, but no one spoke up.

"We'll be on the trail nonstop around four hours before lunch," he went on, "and we'll reach Phantom Ranch a couple hours later." The ranger tipped back his hat and studied the cloudy sky for a moment. "You need to remember two things."

"Drink lots of water," Max mouthed to Karinne.

"One, keep hydrated. It may seem cool right now, but the deeper we descend, the higher the temperatures. There's a twenty-degree difference between the rim and the bottom, even in winter. Use your hats, sunglasses, sunblock, and drink often. This is July, our hottest month. In clear weather it can be more than one hundred and twenty degrees Fahrenheit on the canyon floor."

The other mule wrangler, an attractive woman with long braided hair, spoke next. "That creates another problem. Our mules don't—can't—stop. There are no bathroom facilities for a long time. In ten minutes we mount up. Last chance for you all to make a pit stop. Remember your mule assignment."

"It's single file for humans and mules," the other ranger said. "Mules have the right of way over hikers."

"The trail's *that* narrow?" Karinne exclaimed.

"Yep."

"Good thing they can see all four feet."

More than a few in the group rushed off to the restrooms as Karinne turned to Max.

"Phantom Ranch—that's the stables, right?"

"And the overnight lodgings for riders. We'll meet Cory and Anita there, get our supplies and head downriver tomorrow."

Karinne nodded. She shrugged out of her pack and left it with Max. "Watch this for me? Be back in a minute."

Except it took a lot longer. Karinne ruefully wondered if she should've taken the helicopter, after all, when she saw the line for the ladies' room. The men's room line was no shorter.

Oh, well. Better safe than squirming in the saddle.

When they'd all returned to their mules, the wrangler had everyone mount. She explained that she'd take the point position, and the park ranger would follow in the rear. "Let the mules form their own line after I lead out," she said. "They have their own particular order."

A few minutes of turmoil went by as determined mules took their usual spots. Karinne and Max's mules preferred the end of the trail, with Max's mount positioned directly in front of Karinne's. She adjusted her baseball cap and gave Max a thumbs-up when he turned in his seat to check on her. Then silence set in as the mules took awestruck riders down into the vast colors of the Grand Canyon.

For the first hour Karinne drank in the sights, grateful for the respite from screaming, yelling, drunken crowds that were her work setting day after day. She'd never heard such quiet on the job. And sounds, when she registered them, were soothing, natural. The clop of shod hoofs on packed ground was broken by the occasional screech of a hunting red-tailed hawk—a cry that carried and echoed through the pure air. No trucks or cars or buildings marred the openness—nothing except rock spires and wildlife. Best of all, from Karinne's point of view, this place had Max.

And he'd once offered to give it up for her. How could she allow him to do that? If only she had the courage to quit her own job, but since she couldn't leave her father, it made no sense to leave Phoenix or gainful employment.

After Max graduated from college, he'd discussed his future plans with her. They were a real couple by then, though Karinne was still in school, and Max had reluctantly offered to give up his hopes of a canyon raft concession and continue to do geological work with the city of Phoenix. He'd been hired on, but wasn't happy.

Karinne refused his offer. "No, Max. I'll join you up north when I graduate. I'm sure I can find work in Flagstaff."

After her graduation, they'd been reunited in a Grand Canyon topside hotel. For one happy week the two shared their love, planned their lives together, and Max proposed.

"I wanted to wait until you graduated before making it official," he said, slipping a diamond ring on her finger.

"We'll set a date as soon as I find a job," she promised.

But that promise was derailed when, with Jeff's help, a headhunter tracked her down at the hotel to offer her a media photographer's dream job. She could have refused— would have if Max had objected—but he was silent. So, with hesitation, she accepted.

"I've just finished with classes, and this is a chance of a lifetime," she explained, feeling a little guilty. "I'd like to get some experience for my résumé. Then I'll move up here and we'll get married. It'll only be for a short time."

"As long as it's short," Max replied. In her excitement, Karinne missed hearing the strangeness in his tone.

"It will be. Oh, Dad will be so proud!"

"And so will I," Max said, never reproaching her. Still, the "short time" had turned into months, then years. Her career was so challenging, and then Jeff's heart problems had worsened. There was no sense quitting if she had to stay in Phoenix with her father. Plus she knew Max loved her. He would always be there, and after all, they were still young.

There was another reason Karinne stalled, a secret reason. If Karinne were honest with herself, she was hoping for Margot to reappear. After all, there had never been a body. If she and Jeff moved, how could Margot trace them?

It was wishful thinking, she knew. Foolish, wishful thinking. But all the same, Karinne stayed at home and Max paid the price. He was getting tired of waiting for the family they'd once planned. Karinne would have to harden her heart and do what her father's doctors recommended. That wouldn't be easy. Because selling the family home meant giving up her last hope of finding her mother.

Still... Karinne sighed deeply, a sigh tinged with pleasure that carried clearly in the pristine air. For now, she could shove aside the tedium of constant noise, and even the mystery of a pink sweatshirt and a note signed "Mom."

Max swiveled around in his saddle immediately.

"You okay?" he asked.

Karinne smiled. "Just enjoying the trip."

Max nodded and turned forward again. For the first time since the ride started, the canyon took a backseat in Karinne's vision. Max had an air of caring about him that didn't detract from his masculinity one bit. In fact, she'd always found it one of his most attractive traits. The male athletes she spent her life with were trained to ignore blood and pain, to focus on winning, winning, winning. As the backbone of a multibillion-dollar industry, they were paid exorbitant salaries to do so. No one expected otherwise.

A single sigh would never have signaled such concern from an athlete on the job. Photographers had to suffer the same weather and conditions as the athletes. Even Jeff, her father, had taught her to look after herself, to "be tough" after her mother's death.

With adult hindsight, Karinne often wished she could take back all the "Mom, stop fussing!" complaints she'd made. The "boring" lessons had been signs of a mother's love. Other than for Max, only her mother would have responded so quickly to Karinne's sigh. Strange how one man's action could strike her so deeply.

In certain ways, Max reminded Karinne of the nineteenth-century explorer, John Wesley Powell, whose life she'd studied in American history courses. His studies of the Grand Canyon were not only his life's work, but Powell's personal joy. Powell lived for his expeditions to the Grand Canyon, Green Canyon and the Rocky Mountains.

Karinne studied Max. Of course there were differences, as well. Powell had fought as an army major in the Civil War, losing an arm, which had ended his military career. The Civil War and primitive field medicine had taken its toll on many men, including Powell. The old black-and-white photographs of him hadn't been kind. They showed a determined, too-thin war survivor. He'd refused to give up his passion for exploration and study, even though his expeditions had taken place in a hostile land.

Max Hunter was a successful native of this wild land. Unlike Powell, Max was healthy without the haggard look of early explorers. He moved with an easy masculine grace that Karinne found a pleasant change from the hurly-burly powerhouses on the sports teams. He didn't need weights or vitamins to stay in shape. His skin didn't sport "lucky" tattoos, and his brown hair wasn't streaked, dyed, spiked or shaved in current men's trends. Nor did he have facial piercings and diamond-studded earrings.

Max was her perfect match, except for one thing—geographic compatibility. Togetherness would be hard. The Grand Canyon was one of the most photographed areas in the world, but she couldn't make money there. Nor could she leave her father, not with his heart problem. But lots of people had successful long-distance marriages, including Cory and Anita. Karinne and Max were in love, both committed to making things work, so she'd been happily content...until lately.

Could my mother still be alive? Even the attractive sights and shapes of the canyon around her—including Max Hunter—couldn't distract her. However, she'd try to stay calm. *After all,* she thought, *I'm on vacation....*

FIVE LONG HOURS of riding in intermittent drizzle brought the mules to the Tonto formation. By then, all riders—from first-timers to the more experienced—were ready to dismount and stretch their muscles. The park ranger and wranglers made certain the mules were properly tied to the hitching posts, warned against littering, then checked out the tack while most riders headed for the Porta Potties. Soon after, lunches and drinks were distributed. Karinne and Max both ate their sandwiches standing.

"We're two-thirds of the way there," he said as he noticed Karinne rubbing her shapely behind. "Sore?"

"Not too bad." She dropped her hand and reached into her box lunch for more chips, then fed him one before eating some herself. "Airport lounges and plane seats are worse. At least the sun's out."

Max nodded. "Looks like it might rain again. The air has that feel."

"You'll have to keep me warm tonight," Karinne said, passion sparking in her eyes. "Maybe we can zip our sleeping bags together...."

"I think that can be arranged. I've missed you. I'm tired of missing you."

"We've been together our whole lives," Karinne gently reminded him.

"I'm not talking about living on the same street. I'm talking about being husband and wife. We were childhood friends, and we've done the lovers routine. It's time to take that step forward, become marriage partners."

"I never considered being your lover as routine."

"Isn't that what's it's become, Karinne? You meet me, or I meet you, we catch up on conversation and sex, and separate until the next time."

"That sounds so clinical," she said, uneasy at the tone of his voice.

"You know what I mean," Max said impatiently. "And the worst part is, marriage isn't going to change much. We'll still be stuck in the same rut, unless one of us wants to become unemployed."

"That's the problem with the girl next door. She doesn't always stay there."

Max made no comment. After an uneasy pause, Karinne spoke. "I hope the rain lets up tomorrow. I want to do some hiking."

"Where?"

"Oh, just some of the areas where Powell's expedition took photos. Too bad so many of those pictures didn't survive."

"Some of them did. You should be able to pick up a book in the gift store later." To Karinne's relief, Max sounded like his normal self again. "I've seen them there."

"I planned on it. I especially want to see C. C. Spaulding's work," Karinne said.

"Sorry—I'm not familiar with the name."

"I'm not surprised. He's a mystery man. All that's known of him are his photos. Anyway, Spaulding took a photo in 1906 of an unidentified skeleton. His caption reads 'The Toll.' Supposedly Spaulding found him a few miles below this trail. The person—a white male—had a newspaper dated 1900."

"I know photographers have been shooting the canyon since the 1870s," Max said.

"Yes, but this photo is special. Compositionally, it's a piece of art—and it's an Old West mystery. No one's ever discovered who the man was."

"Are you going to try?"

"No. I have my own mystery to solve." Karinne shook her head, then lifted her chin. *No time like the present.* "Max...the other day, I got a package in the mail. There was a Grand Canyon sweatshirt—pink—inside."

"Pink, huh? That was your favorite color when you were small," he remembered. "You don't wear it much now."

"So you didn't send it?" she asked, not surprised, thinking of the note inside the package. Even so, she wanted Max's opinion on the subject.

"No. You have a secret admirer I don't know about?"

"Hardly." There'd never been anyone for Karinne but Max. As a child, she'd adored the older brother of Cory, her playmate. As a teen, she'd had a crush on the man. As a woman, she loved him and gloried in the knowledge that he loved her back.

"Maybe Cory sent it," Max suggested.

"I doubt it."

Max peered at her. He could always read her moods. "What's wrong? What aren't you telling me?"

"I just wondered who it was really from."

"Wasn't there a card?"

"Yes, but there was no name."

Max frowned. Karinne hesitated to ruin his good mood. This was their first reunion in months. "I'll show it to you later, okay? When I unpack. Right now I'd rather talk about Spaulding."

"Ah." Max seemed satisfied, and Karinne breathed a sigh of relief. She changed the subject to something safer.

"I read about C. C. Spaulding in Dellenbaugh's book, *A Canyon Voyage*. In 1871, when Frederick Dellenbaugh was seventeen, he joined Powell's second canyon expedition. He painted the area."

"Oil paintings, right?"

"Yeah. There was no color film, of course, just black-and-white," Karinne said, warming to her subject. "Oil landscapes were the accepted travel fliers of the day. He traveled all over the world to paint."

"I've seen the book, but I haven't read it," Max said.

"Some editions of his book are illustrated with black-and-white photographs from that same period. Powell had a knack for picking the best men for his expeditions. Perhaps we can retrace some of their footsteps together."

"That's a lot of footsteps." Max smiled. He opened his mouth as she fed him another potato chip.

"I didn't mean *today*. We'll have the rest of our lives to do that."

"I want more time with you than the fits and spurts we get now." Max took her hand and pulled her close for a hug. "I haven't said anything to him yet, but I'd like to make Cory a full partner. Maybe we can hire more workers in a few summers, too. It'll give you and me more time together."

"I'd like that, Max."

"With just the two of us, we can't really take extended breaks. But if we can afford more help, Cory and I could both take more time off. If we can swing it financially, I intend to make it happen," Max said.

Further discussion was curtailed as the park ranger blew his whistle, the prearranged signal for everyone to finish eating and remount.

As the mule train started down the canyon a few minutes

later, Karinne found herself smiling. She hated being apart from Max so much.

And she hated being in the dark about the mysterious pink top. Max hadn't sent it. She'd known it all along but wanted to ask, just in case. And she knew he would never have played a trick like that on her. Besides, Max was alert to all her preferences, and pink wasn't a color she wore much. Like Max, she doubted Cory had bought the top, but she'd ask him tonight at dinner. She didn't want to address any other possibilities until then. For now, she was on vacation and would continue to enjoy it. It didn't matter that a little rain was falling.

THE MULES CONTINUED down to the bottom of the canyon, crossed the suspension bridge across the Colorado and headed for their corral at the Bright Angel Campground. Sunlight faded quickly in the bottoms, although the mile-deep rock sides usually held the day's heat long after the sunlight left. The floor of the Grand Canyon remained a desert environment, even with the monsoon rains far above.

Max turned in his saddle every so often to check on Karinne. She'd seemed a little stressed, but she had an open, welcoming manner about her, so much so that he'd revealed future business plans that he hadn't even discussed with his brother yet. Nor did he feel the need to say, "Please don't tell Cory I want to make him a partner." He knew Karinne possessed sense and tact. She hadn't succeeded in a high-paying, competitive job solely on her father's coattails.

Her knowledge of the area and obvious delight with it impressed him more than he'd let on. As a canyon regular, he was used to the usual moans and groans of tourists. "It's too hot, too cold, too wet" were among the complaints canyon workers had to hear. But like other weekends she'd spent here, Karinne hadn't complained about the men's and women's dorms, where sexes were separated, or the lack of modern restrooms, the cloudy weather, the hard saddles, the no-frills lunch or the normal bodily functions of mules on a trail. Other tourists wrinkled their noses and groaned, finding "outdoor reality" a bit overwhelming. Instead, Karinne accepted the behavior of the mules much as she accepted the behavior of people—with a healthy tolerance that spoke of maturity.

She hadn't had any choice but to grow up after her mother's death. Mr. C had spent more time at home and, when school was out, brought her along on the job and taught her what he knew. A wildlife-photographer father who traveled frequently must have provided a strange upbringing for an only child. With just her widowed father and elderly grandmother, her experience of family was pretty limited.

Max thought uneasily about the last day he'd seen Margot Cavanaugh—and told her he didn't know where her daughter was.

Karinne wasn't the morbid type; she'd accepted her mother's disappearance as the years passed. Max resisted the urge to turn around and check on her once more. A protective, totally male attitude washed over him, and Max gave in to the impulse and glanced at Karinne. Her head tipped back, she took in the brilliant colors directly above her, most of the canyon walls now looming over them. A satisfied smile curved her lips—and his at the sight. He almost felt as if he was on vacation himself. Max looked forward to her first expedition down into the Grand Canyon with more than his usual enthusiasm. They should've made this trip a lot sooner.

The mule train crossed the bridge over the Colorado, the river's surface catching and reflecting the riot of color rising before them. Upriver, the Glen Canyon Dam had slowed much of the river's speed; during heavy rainfall when the dam spill gates were opened, the Colorado was never as untamed as in Powell's days. Max didn't ride the river for cheap white-water thrills. The beauty of the canyon, the wildlife, the old pueblos and cliff dwellings, thousands of archeological sites and the simple pleasure of silently floating down the calmer side tributaries of the river made a far deeper impression than white water could ever provide.

As the mules finished crossing the bridge and headed toward the waiting corrals, Max took one last glance at Karinne to remind himself how lucky he was....

And how glad that there were no phones, no cell service. He didn't have to worry about crank calls here.

MAX AND KARINNE MET up with Cory and Anita in the dining area at Phantom Ranch. Thanks to the brothers' familiarity with the place, the four of them easily secured seats and dinner trays from the buffet.

"How was your chopper ride, Anita?" Karinne immediately asked.

"I loved it! I took some great photos. Nothing like yours, of course." She grinned, patting the pocket where she kept her camera. "But enough to wow my friends at work when I go back to visit."

Karinne gave Anita a thumbs-up. "That's the spirit."

"Make 'em all jealous," Cory said between mouthfuls of roasted chicken.

"I love it here," Anita said.

"You both could stay longer," Cory offered, surprising them all. "We have the provisions."

"I can stay as long as I want. I'm ready to look for work here," Anita said happily as she kissed Cory on the cheek. "I'm free as a bird, except for Karinne and Max's wedding. Hard to believe it's only a few months away."

"I know," Karinne said, seated next to Max. She leaned her head on his shoulder for a second. "I'm the bride, re-member?"

Anita scanned the crowd. "Good thing we got a table."

"I've seen worse." Max buttered his corn on the cob. "Summer holidays are always horrendous."

"Especially the Fourth of July weekend," Cory agreed. "Now *that's* a mob."

"No," Karinne said. "For terrible crowds, try Super Bowl Sunday. I remember one game when I couldn't hear out of my headphones, and I had them on full blast. I've had it with noise and chaos. That's why I wanted a small, quiet wedding. As long as everyone we've invited shows up, we'll be happy."

"I'll be there," Anita said.

Soon afterward, their plates cleared, Anita rose to go to her room.

"I'll walk you there," Max volunteered.

Cory and Karinne stayed behind to finish their coffee.

"Want dessert?" Cory asked.

"No, thanks. I'm full."

"Same here. Wanna go?"

"Just a second. I've got a quick question," she said. "Did you send me a Grand Canyon sweatshirt last week?"

"A sweatshirt?"

"In the mail—a hooded pink one."

"Not me."

"I wish I knew who did," Karinne muttered. "It's been bugging me."

"Was there a note?" Cory asked.

"Y-yes."

"And?"

Karinne hesitated, then decided to tell him. She and

Cory were close, and Max had unexpectedly left with Anita.

"It was signed 'Mom.'"

"Dammit!" Cory swore. "That's not funny, Karinne."

"No, it isn't. It all started when I took this photo of someone who looked like my mother." She went on to explain, Cory's eyes serious as he listened to her story.

"And you went to the police when the sweatshirt came in the mail?"

"I did after I took the picture." Karinne shrugged. "Max doesn't know."

"You'd better tell him," Cory said.

"I plan on it. But he's already upset enough. He's worried that we won't be able to spend any more time together when we're married than we do now."

"I can believe it," Cory said. "What do you expect? It takes both me and Max to run the expeditions. I'm in the same boat with Anita when she's working."

"Yes, but this was the first time he didn't act excited about the wedding. He wasn't…himself. I didn't want to say anything about Mom to him."

"Does Anita know about this? The note? The sweatshirt?"

Karinne shook her head. "No. She has enough to worry about, losing her job and all."

"I don't think she's that upset about losing her job anymore. And if she is, I'll make it up to her," Cory said with a sexy smirk. "Long-distance marriages are for the birds. I don't know how military wives or husbands stand it."

"They don't have a choice. Like me."

"You're wrong. You do have a choice, Karinne. You just refuse to see it."

Karinne shifted uneasily in her seat and decided

not to comment on Cory's observation. She steered the conversation back to the earlier topic.

"You don't believe my mother's alive, do you?" she asked.

"No way."

"Dad didn't, either. But I have a feeling—"

"Wishful thinking."

"We've always been straight with each other, Cory. If you were me, what would you do?"

"I wouldn't take any chances with a deranged stalker," he said.

"Why would anyone stalk me? I'm no celebrity."

"Still, you shouldn't set yourself up as target for some creepy con artist."

"I don't intend to...but I thought I'd wear the top," Karinne blurted out.

Cory ran his hand through his hair. "But we just agreed that your mother's dead."

"Yes..." Karinne took in a deep breath. "If by some miracle she isn't...wearing it would be a signal, wouldn't it? Like a green light saying I'm approachable."

"Skip the green lights for anyone but Max," Cory said. "Forget about this woman—and go back to flower arrangements for the wedding. Guest lists. Whatever."

"I still have to tell Max."

Cory swore. Karinne stared at him in frank amazement. "Sorry." Cory piled his tray with the empty dishes and glasses. "It's just that the same thing's been happening to Max."

"What?"

"He's been getting crank calls from someone who claims to be your mother."

"Why didn't he *tell* me?" At Cory's raised eyebrows,

she winced. "I know—I'm guilty of the same thing." She frowned. "Did he go to the police?"

"Yes, but he learned nothing. You two need to talk."

Karinne nodded. "This trip's off to a great start."

"Tell him," Cory ordered, throwing down his napkin and rising. "Now's as good a time as any." He gestured toward Max, who was returning to their table. "See you later."

Karinne sipped her coffee as Max rejoined her. "I showed Anita where the women's dorms are, where you and she will be staying tonight."

"Dorms…" Karinne groaned with dismay. "Too bad they don't have a real hotel down here. Or someplace we could share a sleeping bag."

"That's the story of our life, isn't it? Never together."

Karinne shivered. "Don't say never."

Max pointed at her coffee. "Are you ready to go?"

"Not yet." She set down her mug. "I wanted to talk to you about a photo I took a few months ago. There was this woman…" She told Max everything that had happened back at the stadium and her visit to the police station.

"I even told Dad about it, but he didn't buy it."

A long pause seemed to fill the air. The other diners faded into the background. Max's expression seemed so serious Karinne shivered.

"I may have heard from that woman, too," he finally said.

"Cory told me," Karinne whispered. "And she claimed to be my mother?"

"Yes."

A million questions jumped into her mind. She asked the easiest one. "When was this?"

"Almost two months ago. After we put our engagement announcement in the paper. A woman called. Said she was Margot and wanted to wish us well."

Karinne shivered again, despite the hot coffee. "Why didn't you tell me before?"

"Because the Flagstaff police and park rangers thought it was a crank call. So did I."

"That's what the Phoenix police told *me*. But obviously this goes beyond that. You should've said something," she insisted.

"And you, too."

She bowed her head in acknowledgment. "You don't think…my mother could be alive, do you?"

"No."

"I wish the woman had called me instead of you," Karinne said. "I would've recognized the voice if it really was Mom."

"I'm glad she didn't. I'd hate to think she had your phone number. Or worse, your address," Max said.

"This person *does* have my address," Karinne admitted miserably. "She sent me a Grand Canyon sweatshirt—and a note."

"Someone actually sent you a package? When?"

"Last week. This woman wants to see me."

Max's eyes darkened with concern. "Go on."

"I threw the whole package out. But then I fished it out of the trash and brought the top with me. I thought maybe…I should wear it."

"Why?"

"As…a signal, in case Mom *is* alive. To let her know I'm approachable."

"Don't encourage this craziness! That's the last thing you want!"

"That's what Cory said."

"You've talked to Cory about this, and not me?" he asked angrily.

Karinne flushed. "Just a few minutes ago. And don't

lecture me, Max. You told Cory about your incident with this strange woman. *Cory,* not me."

"Point taken." He sighed. "In future, we have to be more forthright with each other."

"Then I'll say it right out. I want to follow this and see where it leads."

"What's next? A stalker crashing the wedding?"

Karinne shook her head. "I don't think this woman wants to hurt me. She's respected my privacy so far."

"That's not how I see it."

"And pink used to be my favorite color…."

"Yours and a million other little girls'."

"Still, if there's a chance—any chance—my mother's alive, I want to know."

"Let me play devil's advocate. Say Margot *is* alive. You'd want a sick person like that in your life? Someone who faked her own suicide and put you and your father through hell? *If* she's alive, which I doubt."

"Max, we can't be sure."

"Exactly. Something to think about before welcoming a Trojan horse." He reached across the table for her hand. "Come on, there are others waiting for this table. Let's go."

Outside, the long shadows from the walls and spires of the canyon crisscrossed Phantom Ranch. Most of the park visitors were eating or in the dorms using the communal showers. Max and Karinne found a bench where they could have some privacy. They sat side by side, Max's arm around her shoulders.

"I was hoping to have a nice, quiet vacation where I could concentrate just on us," Karinne told him.

"I'll settle for a nice, quiet wedding," Max said. "How's your father taking all this?"

Karinne sat up and pushed the hair back from her face.

"Better than I am. He seemed to shrug it off, but he didn't totally convince me. We never had proof Mom was actually dead. Deep down, I suspect he keeps hoping Mom will come home. That's why he's never sold the house and moved into a retirement community. I guess I felt that way, too. That's why I didn't leave Phoenix after college."

The cold steel in Max's eyes disturbed her. "Even though we were seriously involved by then?"

"I wanted to stay near our home base."

"And all this time, I thought you stayed in Phoenix for your career."

"I— It—it was both…" Karinne stammered.

"So you're telling me that you're pinning the future of our marriage on your father's unrealistic hopes for Margot's return—and yours. That your loyalties lie with your mother first, then your father, then me?"

"You're twisting my words!"

"I don't think I am. This isn't fair to either of us, Karinne. It's one thing for you to stay in Phoenix because of your father's age and health, not that I ever thought he needed a babysitter. But this—this is…"

For the first time ever, Karinne saw Max at a loss for words.

"Max, you don't understand!"

"I understand that I love you. Do you love me?"

"Of course I do!"

His eyes narrowed. "Here's my next question. If they'd found your mother's body years ago, if you weren't waiting for her to turn up at your old home, would you and I be together? Here at the Grand Canyon?"

"You know my job's based in Phoenix."

"That's not an answer." His arm dropped from her shoulders as he swiveled to meet her gaze. "Let me rephrase the question. Is it your job keeping you in Phoenix, or is it some fantasy about Margot?"

"Fantasy?" she echoed.

"Don't be a coward, Karinne. At least have the guts to answer my question."

On the outside, Karinne didn't flinch from his harsh voice. On the inside, she told herself to tread carefully.

"My job is what it is," she said calmly. "As for my mother, if she's alive, she'd want to be at the wedding. *I'd* want her to be at the wedding."

Max said nothing.

"I hope all this can be settled by then."

"Realistically, it may not be," he said. "You have to accept that. This is probably a wild-goose chase."

"I know, but if she's alive, I'd like to see her again."

"That's extremely generous, considering the circumstances. If this woman *is* your mother, you realize it means she really did abandon you and your father. Are you okay with that?"

Karinne frowned. "No, but there's nothing I can do to change the past. And Mom might need me. Maybe that's why she's turned up after all these years."

"And that's why you're okay with us having a long-distance marriage. Because Jeff—or your *mother*—might need you."

"Not exactly, but…"

"What about what *we* need?"

"Max, we've been through this before. You can't work in Phoenix, and I'm always on the road, no matter where my home base is. Once I can talk my father into moving into a retirement home and out of that big house…maybe I could move to Flagstaff. I need to be near an airport."

"Jeff's never going to move as long as he has you in the

palm of his hand, Karinne. He lost Margot, and he's held on to you ever since."

"It won't be forever."

"How long, Karinne? One year? Ten? Twenty?"

Karinne kissed him. "You know I love you."

"That doesn't fix anything."

"No. But this is the first time I've been here longer than a weekend—the first time we've been together on the river. Can't we just enjoy it for now?"

Max sighed heavily.

"I wish we weren't sleeping in dorms tonight. I wish we were in our own tent, just you and me," Karinne murmured.

"If nothing else, we won't be getting strange phone calls and packages," he replied. "Come on, I'll walk you to the women's dorms. Tomorrow morning we'll catch a chopper up the river to Lee's Ferry, unload our gear and raft the eighty-seven miles back here to Phantom Ranch."

Chapter Five

Mile Zero,
Lee's Ferry, Colorado River

THEY SLOWLY DRIFTED down the Colorado River, a steady rain muting the brilliant colors of the canyon into softer pastels. The inflatable raft, loaded with supplies, bobbed on the surface of the Colorado. These calmer waters were noisily pitted by rain that made conversation harder, but not impossible. Sound was amplified by the sides of Marble Canyon, a pseudo-marble section of the Grand Canyon with smooth, polished walls of rock.

Max rode in the back, using the engine tiller but no power to navigate, while Karinne and Anita sat on the sides and simply watched, letting the current take the raft downstream. Dangerous rapids were nonexistent in this part of the canyon. Cory sat in the bow, looking out for boulders. She and Anita also practiced with the paddles in this slower area. So far, the women had done well as paddlers, despite the poor visibility. The raft carried four oars.

"This is such a beautiful place," Karinne said. "If only there wasn't so much traffic." Far ahead of them other craft floated, while behind them a large pontoon boat with more than a dozen tourists carefully negotiated the bends.

The canyon walls loomed upward, their colors distorted by the rain, the color bands merging up toward the rims with a shimmering fluidity. It never presented the same vista twice, yet each different panorama provided a magnificent, raw beauty as timeless as the waters that ran beneath their raft.

"The canyon has as many moods as days of the year," Max remarked. "You should've brought your cameras."

"I don't think my cameras could do justice to this," Karinne said. "They couldn't capture it, not even with a wide-angle lens." She gestured to the towering splendor, her head craned back as she gazed up at the riot of colors. "And certainly not in one trip."

"Or in one season," Max added. "Which is why we get a lot of repeat business. People who come once can't wait to see it again."

"It has a wild uniqueness all its own," Karinne agreed. "I can see why you never tire of it."

"Max can really wax poetic," Cory said, "but he's right. And here comes more rain…"

"I hate monsoon season." Anita huddled into the yellow rain slicker.

Karinne, on the other hand, had thrown back her head, pulled her rain-spotted sunglasses off and continued to take in the beauty on either side of the river. She caught Max's eye, and smiled.

By midmorning the rain had stopped, and conversation became easier. The party of four had traveled through limestone and sandstone walls.

"Break time—Mile 4.5," Max announced.

"How can you tell?" Karinne asked. She'd seen only a few mile markers.

Max pointed upward. "The Navajo bridges—old and new."

Above them spanned the old 1929 Navajo bridge and, at its side, the new bridge, connecting North Rim to South Rim.

"And here I thought you had some clever trick up your sleeve," Karinne said, grinning as Max and Cory pulled the raft ashore.

"Who's ready for coffee?" Cory asked, helping the women out as Max unloaded a portable gas burner.

"Can we do a real fire?" Anita shivered. Her clothes, especially her jeans, were wet below the slicker.

"My sneakers are sloshing," Karinne seconded.

"We won't have a fire until tonight. We have to prestack fuel for fires," Max said. "Change clothes if you want. Hopefully the sun will be out soon."

"I'm glad this isn't a photo session," Karinne said happily. "I can just *enjoy* it." She let Max pull her close and hugged him back. They kissed gently, mindful of the others.

He brushed the hair from her forehead. "Where are we?" she murmured.

"Still in Marble Canyon," Max said.

"Feels good to stand." The riverbed pebbles crunched under their wet shoes as they stretched their legs.

"Let's see if you feel the same later on. We have rapids coming up."

"So soon?" Anita asked, overhearing them.

"Badger Rapid, Mile 8," Cory said. "Named after an explorer who made badger stew there."

"But the alkaline water turned the animal fat into soap. Hence, Soap Creek Rapid, right after Mile 11." Max spoke with a guide's practiced ease, his arm firmly around Karinne's waist.

"I'll pass on eating badger," Karinne said. "But the rapids should be fun."

"As long as we stay in the boat," Cory warned.

"Wise words," Max said. "The white water is tricky here. Cory and I will steer. If you go overboard, don't try to push off from the rocks or fight the current. Just concentrate on getting air, and you'll beach down below. We'll find you."

"We've never lost a customer," Cory said, reassuring Anita, who looked a little nervous. "And we'll have calm water for a bit."

The four stood and gratefully drank their coffee, warming themselves until Max ushered them back into the raft.

"Ahh...here comes the sun." Karinne took out her sunglasses with the sports strap as the miles of multihued rising cliffs and shoreline boulders heated and baked the humidity, first into steam, then into air. The smoother waters calmed her nerves, as did the company of the others, particularly Max, but the mist seemed unsettling.

"We're rafting through shale now," Max said. "Keep an eye open for prehistoric fern and insect fossils. After a heavy rain, you can easily see the exposed ones in the rocks."

Karinne spotted the first fossil—and Anita whipped out her digital camera to snap some shots.

"Badger and Jackass Canyons coming up," Cory sang out. "Ladies, stow your paddles and hang on."

"Badger's on the right, Jackass on the left. The rapids form where their streams empty. Check your life jackets, and hold on tight," Max warned. "Remember, if you fall out, don't fight the current. Keep your arms close to your body. Just let the current take you into the calmer waters and wait for us."

"I'm *not* going swimming today," Karinne insisted. "You ready, Anita?"

"As ready as I'm going to be." Anita held tight to her straps.

"I'm right here." Cory met Anita's gaze, then turned to face the rapids.

The Colorado River frothed more white than dark as the side canyon stream tumbled into the main body of river water.

Karinne heard Anita gasp as Max and Cory expertly guided the raft though the obstacles. Karinne laughed, her spirits lifting. She felt as if she was on nature's greatest roller coaster, bouncing up and down, her sunglasses spattered, her grasp secure on the raft's handles. When they finally emerged into calmer waters, Karinne felt happier for the experience.

"Everyone okay?" Max asked.

"Still breathing," Anita replied. She seemed to have lost much of her nervousness.

"Great," Karinne said, pulling down her life jacket, which had crawled up in the roughness of the water. "In fact, I could do that again."

"You will. Soap Creek Rapid is three miles down," Max told them.

"Are you ladies still warm?" Cory asked.

"Warm enough, I guess," Karinne said.

"Okay, then, we'll just bail and keep on going."

The water had soaked everyone from head to toe, despite the women's slickers. The men, who rarely bothered with them on the river, untied the plastic folding buckets and passed them to the women to bail water. The inflated raft wouldn't sink, but navigation would be easier without the extra water weight downriver. For this trip, Max shut off the motor, which he'd used for the rapids. The current alone would propel them.

"I wonder if I should become a river guide," Anita said suddenly. "Accounting is starting to seem awfully dull."

"Frankly, I never thought of you as the guide type, Anita," Karinne said as the men continued to navigate.

"I think she'd do all right," Cory said.

"I need a job. Why *not* join Cory?" Anita asked.

Karinne stopped bailing. The thought of being with Max around the clock was a heaven impossible to imagine, not with the children Max always said he wanted. Or maybe Cory had a point. Maybe she hadn't *allowed* herself to imagine it.

"Before we hit the rapids in a few minutes, watch the shale and sandstone. It dates back to the Pennsylvanian Period. Here the layers are full of reptile fossils. You should be able to see them."

The women nodded, studying the various rocks. The layered rock and cross-bedded formations glistened in the steaming humidity fogging off the walls.

"I can picture this as a primordial mist," Karinne said. "And dinosaurs are wading around the next bend. Max, can we hike around the fossil beds?"

"For preservation purposes, it's not allowed. Sorry," Max said as Karinne sighed in disappointment. "But the next time we stop, it'll be for the day. We'll do the House Rock Rapid, then the Roaring 20s before pitching the tents," Max said.

"What are the Roaring 20s?" Anita asked.

"Mile 20.5 through Mile 27 is all rapids," Max explained, taking in the other watercraft about them. "Hence, the Roaring 20s. We'll camp around Mile 32. We'll stop early enough to beat the crowd and get a good campsite."

"We have trail bars if you get hungry before then," Cory offered. "Plus a big dinner and campfire stories afterward."

"I love ghost stories… How about you, Karinne?" Anita teased.

Karinne thought of C. C. Spauldings's "The Toll"—the nameless skeleton in an old photograph—and wondered how the family of the deceased man had lived the rest of their lives without closure, without details. All of a sudden, one pink sweatshirt and a note had put her back in that category.

"I'm not in the mood for ghost stories," Karinne said honestly. She hadn't told Anita about the note from the woman claiming to be her mother.

"Karinne?" Max asked. "You okay?"

She wasn't. That photo had reminded Karinne of her mother and set off strange dreams. Something about that image—the lost soul, the pathetic skeleton faceup by the side of the water—had upset her, despite her professional interest. It represented the loss of a family member, perhaps someone's parent. Someone like Margot.

Suddenly, she didn't look forward to the evening campfire with her usual enthusiasm. She felt uncharacteristically uneasy, definitely unsettled. Her smile back to Max felt weak in response. She settled herself safely into the raft, checked her life jacket and grabbed at her safety loops.

"I'll be fine once we get through those rapids."

The water current pushed the raft ahead. Max restarted the engine for additional power and began the journey. The men steered through the turbulence, but Karinne couldn't get into the spirit of the ride.

Anita's exhilaration showed. She even cheered, "Faster!" as the large silver pontoon raft behind was catching up to them.

With its larger engine and heavier weight, the pontoon raft traveled faster through the rapids than the smaller raft, and soon gained on them. Max and Cory also noticed the approach of the pontoon with its dozen passengers.

"They're getting awfully close to us!" Cory yelled out, making corrections with his paddle.

"I see them!" Max yelled back.

"What do we do?" Anita asked.

"The bigger boat has the right of way," Max said. "Don't worry—we're fine."

Their smaller raft certainly seemed more maneuverable, Karinne decided, holding on tightly. The Colorado River could easily accommodate both craft, even in the rock- and rapid-strewn areas. Karinne watched the approach of the silver pontoon with its passengers whooping at the impromptu race. The pontoon pulled beside them, white water showering everyone, but both captains could see well enough to maneuver.

The pontoon's pilot yelled a friendly greeting to Max, then began to pull ahead. Karinne blinked. One older gentleman in the raft was actually snapping pictures with both hands! Karinne sat up straight, admiring the nerve of the photographer, and wondered if he was a professional or hobbyist. She dashed water from her eyes and squinted, trying to get a better look at the camera, when she suddenly noticed the woman directly behind him.

Another splash beneath the smaller raft lifted them into the air, and for a moment Karinne was exactly level with the woman. It wasn't just *any* woman—it was her mother....

Older, a little heavier, but Karinne knew that face. The woman turned her head, giving Karinne a full frontal view instead of a profile. Their eyes met. Karinne gasped in shock and her fingers loosened on the straps, just as a huge powerful plume of water hit her in the chest and swept her overboard.

As her back slapped against the water, she thought

she heard the woman call out her name, but Max's voice drowned it out. The icy water sent chills up and down her body, the current kicked her about. The force spun, bounced and haphazardly dragged her through the rapids. Then she lost sight of the yellow raft and the silver pontoon. She almost panicked. She bobbed up again and managed to catch a glimpse of Max.

"Hang on," he shouted. "We're coming!"

She felt his strength become hers and wrapped her vulnerable arms around her life jacket, letting the Colorado take her, its human cork, wherever it pleased. The cold felt unbearable as Karinne fought for air in the maelstrom. Suddenly, she found herself caught in an eddy, whirling around and around the edges. It seemed almost alive as it tried to pull her down into the murkiness of the deeper waters. Karinne kicked hard, using her arms, desperately struggling to keep away from the eddy and the hidden rocks beneath it. Despite the life jacket, she felt her strength failing as the sucking current pulled at her feet.

"Karinne!" Max yelled. "Stop fighting! Hold your breath and let it take you under!"

Karinne couldn't see his face, nor could she see the yellow of the raft or the silver of the pontoon.

"It'll bring you up again! Go down!"

Let the water take her down? Karinne kicked even harder, trying to break free.

"Take a breath and just let go!" Max ordered.

"We'll find you, I promise!" Cory yelled.

"Do it, Karinne!" Anita screamed.

Karinne could hear the panic in Anita's voice. She realized she might sink—drown—right now. She was running out of strength in the limb-chilling spray and it was becoming harder and harder to fight for air pockets in the white water.

"Now, Karinne! While you still can! If we get separated, the other boat will pick you up!"

Karinne choked and sputtered. She didn't know the Colorado. She couldn't understand how Max could trust such a rogue river, but she trusted Max—and she wasn't about to lose her future with him now.

She allowed herself another few seconds to suck in air. In between sprays of white water she gulped as deep as she could and, with one final shiver, let herself go down into the sucking maelstrom. The water pulled her under with a strength that threatened to tear the sneakers off her feet. She felt the heaviness of deeper water pressing down on her, the buoyancy of her body and life jacket no match for its weight. Then, with a rib-crushing torrent, the current caught at her one last time to throw her upward into the air, the light, and into view of the glorious yellow raft captained by the man she loved, waiting just as he'd promised.

But even as she swam toward safety, her mind reeled with old images, and new ones.

That woman in the other raft... Could it be...her mother?

Chapter Six

Karinne still felt queasy with fear and adrenaline. She also felt incredibly foolish for falling into the river and not following Max's directions. Eventually, she'd let the current grab her, take her under and bring her back to the surface of the Colorado.

Max and Anita had pulled her inside the raft. Cory soon docked at the closest camping area downriver. Max hadn't left Karinne since they'd arrived on the shore and he'd helped her out. He threw a dry towel around her shoulders, briskly rubbing them, and making her feel like a two-year-old instead of the confident woman she usually was.

"Are you okay?" Anita asked.

Karinne nodded.

"Cory, why don't you start a fire?" Max suggested. "Come on, Karinne, time to get out of those wet clothes."

A few minutes later, she entered the Porta Potti with dry clothing and a replacement pair of socks. She refused to give in to the urge to be sick to her stomach—an urge not related to the potent odor of chemical treatment—and, once she'd changed clothes, hurried outside again, the door flapping closed behind her.

Karinne took in the Porta Potti door and read the sign posted to prevent campers and wild animals from close contact. It read *For Safety and Hygiene, Please Latch This Door Securely!* With trembling fingers, Karinne tried to fasten the outside catch. She couldn't. The cold, her nerves and aftershock made it impossible. And she'd left her soggy wet mass of clothes inside on the wooden floor. Max got them and closed the door latch for her.

"This place has more rules than a courthouse," she said, trying to make a joke. Her voice shook.

"Come on, sit down."

"We can't." Karinne gestured to another sign in front of bubbling springs and the garden of ferns, mosses and flowers to the far right.

Please Do Not Approach! Protected Area For Endangered Kanab Ambersnails.

"I thought we'd sit over here." Max guided her to an area where a weatherworn wooden bench allowed visitors to lounge safely behind the edge of the springs' boundaries, the water itself surrounded by saddleback-shaped boulders, rubbed smooth by thousands of years of erosion. Karinne sat while Max dropped her wet clothes onto one of the rocks and joined her on the bench. He put his arm around her and drew her close.

"Warmer?" he asked.

"Drier, anyway." She couldn't help shivering.

"Cory'll start a fire," Max assured her. "What happened out there?" he asked.

"I fell," Karinne replied.

"I checked the hand loop. It's fine. Did you lose your balance?"

"No, I just…didn't hold on."

"That's not like you, Karinne."

"I got distracted."

"Hold tighter next time." He urged her even closer.

"I will. Promise me you won't think I'm crazy." At his nod, Karinne gulped in a deep breath.

"I thought I saw my mother."

"Here?"

"In the silver pontoon. Max, it looked like her. I swear it was Mom again. I twisted to see better. That's when I fell in."

"You scared the hell out of me," Max said.

"I scared myself more." Despite her dry clothes, she shivered again. "You never told me about the whirlpools. I'm starting to hate surprises. How can you live in a place like this, Max?"

"First of all, you said you wanted to see what I did for a living. Second, if you weren't chasing a ghost, you wouldn't have fallen out of the raft. Your obsession with the past could've cost you your life! You didn't follow the rules, you just jumped head over heels—literally—for a stranger in another raft. I thought you had more sense than that."

Karinne leaped to her feet, away from the rock and out of his arms. "So I'm an idiot?"

"No, *I'm* the idiot. Because from now on, I'm going to do everything I can to help you find this woman."

"You will? Oh, Max!"

"And then, after that, you're going to choose between having a husband or chasing after your parents the rest of your life. I want to live mine with you. If it isn't going to be that way, I want to know by the end of this trip."

"You're really giving me an ultimatum?" Karinne gasped.

"No, I'm giving myself one. This is our last chance to see if our relationship can work. I love you, Karinne, but if I can't have you in my life—and so far I haven't—it's time to cut our losses."

"I've been with you every chance I get!"

"A weekend every few months? That's not enough. You know my father was a cruise-ship captain, and Mom and Cory and I were always without him. I hated it. I swore I'd never do that to my own family. I offered to move to Phoenix once, and you told me not to. The ball's in your court. It's time for you to make up your mind."

"And what about you?" she accused. "You keep saying you want children. Do you expect me to quit my job? I could, you know. But I just don't see the point. You think we'll see each other more with me and the babies at home and you rafting down the Colorado? I might as well be working."

Now it was Max's turn to gasp. "You don't want children? But you always said…"

"Yes, I do, but under normal conditions. I'd end up with the same thing your mom had. An absentee husband. There's no day care on the river. Or if you stopped working and I continued, it would be the same thing. I'd be an absentee mother and wife. Why subject the children to what we already suffered through?"

His voice grew grim, cold. "So you're saying marriage wouldn't change anything?"

"I didn't say that." Karinne rubbed her forehead. "But sometimes I don't know what to think."

"Make up your mind. I want to know where this relationship stands."

"It's where it's always been! With me loving you!" she said hoarsely.

"It's not enough, Karinne. It's not."

"YOU THINK SHE'S all right?" Anita asked, glancing over her shoulder at Max and Karinne in the distance as Cory started arranging wood.

"If dry clothes and a fire don't do the trick, Max will."

Anita sank to her knees to join him, her arms filled with wood. "She could've *drowned*."

"Not with us on the job," Cory said. "Sooner or later she'd have tired, and the current would have moved her clear. The smart thing is to do it willingly, without panicking."

Anita shivered. "It seemed like forever."

"But everything's fine." Cory took out his waterproof matches.

"I'm so glad. What would we have told her father?" Anita dropped her wood. She covered her face with both hands.

"Anita?" Instantly Cory was at her side. "Hey, it's okay." He gently patted her shaking shoulders.

"Sorry."

"Don't be," Cory said. "You're Karinne's friend. Nothing wrong with that." He retrieved his bandanna from her soggy jeans pocket, then pulled her hand down from her cheek to press it into her palm. "I nearly had a heart attack myself."

"You did?" Anita sniffed.

"For a minute there, I thought Max was going to jump in after her, which would've been no help at all. The look on his face..." Cory shuddered. "Anyway, don't let this scare you out of the raft. Max and I know what we're doing. We don't risk the really nasty rapids."

"That wasn't the worst?" Anita asked in a shaky voice.

"Not the deluxe thrill package. And you wanted to be a river guide," Cory teased.

"Maybe I'll find an accountant's job topside," Anita said.

"Either way, we can relax for the rest of the day," Cory assured her. "Let everyone catch their breath."

"Shouldn't we go check on Karinne?"

"Wait for the coffee to heat first."

Anita watched Cory finish with the wood. "Where are we, anyway?"

"Mile 32—well, 31.9, to be exact. George Vasey's Paradise."

"Oh."

"Come on, mop your face, and ask me who he was," Cory coaxed.

Anita wiped her cheeks with the bandanna. "Who was Vasey?"

"A botanist. He and Powell were together for the 1868 expedition to the Colorado River. Nice place, isn't it? Karinne could've picked a worse spot to fall out," Cory said.

The maidenhair fern blended with the flowers in a fantastic array no florist could ever duplicate. Moss gently hugged the springs, creating emerald surfaces on rock and below the waterline.

"The snails must love it here," Cory said. "They're supposedly descendants from the Late Pleistocene species. Still got your camera?"

Anita pulled out her digital camera, took it out of the zippered plastic bag and snapped a few photos.

After a moment Cory said, "I should finish the fire and get the coffee going. You wanna stay here?"

"No, I'll help."

Cory extended his hand and pulled her to her feet. "Back to the real world, then."

The four of them reunited at the campsite.

"Why don't we set up the tents and you ladies start dinner?" Max suggested, his voice cold. Cory gave his brother a questioning look, but Max didn't respond.

"Karinne, you up to it?" Anita asked.

"Of course." Karinne's voice shook slightly. "I just took a dunking. I didn't get hurt."

The women unpacked the cooking gear, then set up water to boil for pasta—a light-to-carry food stock.

"Want to hear a ghost story before dinner?" she asked Anita quietly. "I've got one."

"You don't want to wait for the guys?"

"Trust me—*this* story they've already heard."

Karinne soon related her tale, as Anita marveled at the turn of events. She didn't mention the part about Max wanting to end their relationship. He couldn't be serious. Perhaps it was just the stress of the moment.

"How can you stand it? Either your mother's alive or some creep is stalking you. No wonder you fell out of the raft. I'd be a wreck."

"I am," Karinne admitted. "I don't need to wait for dark to feel nervous."

"And I thought you had a rough day falling out of the boat," Anita exclaimed, stirring in uncooked spaghetti.

"Now I'll have to find a new roommate. Once you move out here…life won't be the same," Karinne said sadly.

"We'll see each other."

"Not often enough. You'll be with Cory, and I'll be stuck with some new roommate who leaves dishes in the sink and pays her rent late. Are you serious about joining Max and Cory?" Karinne asked.

Anita shrugged. "I don't know enough to be a guide, but I'm tired of not being with my husband. Why are things so complicated?"

LATER, IN THE TENT with Max, Anita's words echoed in her head. Instead of the double sleeping bag with Max, they each lay alone in their single bags. Karinne broke the silence first.

"Anita wanted to know why life's so complicated," she said to Max.

His expression was unreadable in the dark. He ran his hand through his hair. "Are you speaking generally or specifically? Either way, I don't have answers."

Karinne tried again. "Do you really think Anita could be a guide?"

"It depends. There's a lot she'd have to learn, but if she really wanted to, I don't see why not. Cory's a good teacher."

"I doubt she could find an accounting job topside in Grand Canyon Village," Karinne said. "Maybe in Flagstaff, but she still couldn't live in the same place with Cory."

"Is that what she wants to do?" Max asked.

"She doesn't know. I do know she'd prefer her husband to her roommate. And I'd rather live with you." She took a deep breath. "Did you really mean what you said back there? That we're through?"

"Yes."

"But…" She willed her voice to stay calm. "Why?"

"You know why. You want all or nothing, you always have. And between your job and your family, *I'm* left with nothing. The way things are going, I won't have children." His tone betrayed a deep disappointment she hated to hear. "There's no future in this. The one time I offered to move to Phoenix, you resisted."

"I didn't want you to resent me."

"But you don't want to move up here."

"I don't want to resent you."

Max propped himself up on one elbow and looked down at her. "No, you don't want to make a commitment to me. To anyone. I used to think you did—that you had—but we keep getting older and nothing changes. You've planned three weddings, only to cancel two of them. I don't think this one will be any different. You'll use your search for your mother as an excuse to postpone or cancel. How long will that take, Karinne?"

"If this is some prank, it won't take any time at all."

"And if it isn't? If Margot is alive? How much further away do I get pushed?"

"I...I..."

"You don't know. Of course you don't. I'm not even surprised anymore. Just—resigned."

Karinne paused, the darkness in the tent suddenly ominous. "What do you mean?"

"Well..." he said slowly. "Even when we're married, it seems the most we'll ever have is the occasional meeting. Like this. We've been together for years, yet this is the first time you've ever showed any real interest in the canyon."

"I've been working."

"You've been working, there's your father and now suddenly you've dragged your mother into the picture."

"I love my father. And my mother. And you."

"I'm always at the end of your list, Karinne. Always."

"If that were true, I wouldn't be sharing a tent with you!"

"You came here because you had to use your vacation time. And to make arrangements for yet another pretend wedding."

"I came because I care. Do you really want to waste the little time we have together arguing?"

"I don't want to argue at all. We're finished, Karinne. I've loved you forever, but I want more. When this trip is over, when this mystery is solved and I know you're safe, we're over."

"So does that mean we still can make love?"

"I'm not in the mood, Karinne."

Desperate, she leaned toward his lips and kissed him. "I can get you in the mood."

Max didn't kiss her back.

"Enough," he said. "I don't want to be with a little girl. Deep down, that's all you are, Karinne. A little girl still hoping for her mother to come home. I can't wait any longer for you to grow up. I won't."

THE MORNING SUN rose in the east, sending shafts of light down through the canyon. The light flashed off the Colorado and bounced off the colored canyon spires, splintering into rays and projecting thin shadows on the walls. Despite the cheery morning, the four campers got a late start. Other watercraft were already under way when Max and Cory finally launched the raft, the women seated within, the gear tightly fastened and neatly stowed.

Karinne didn't even try to stifle her yawn, despite both hands on her paddle. Sleep had been a long time coming, and when she finally did drop off, she hadn't slept well. She couldn't believe Max had broken off their relationship. She'd tossed and turned. She'd had nightmares about Max leaving her at the altar. Then she'd dreamed of her mother.

Never would she have imagined that Max would have such doubts and end their engagement. At least he'd promised to stay with her to see this through. She hoped that would be enough time for her to make things right between them. Nor could she have guessed that he'd have had contact with the "ghost." If by some miracle Margot Cavanaugh was alive, what would Karinne's father say? Would Karinne be able to get beyond feeling angry and cheated? And would Max be able to see past another distraction interfering with his and Karinne's relationship?

Karinne wanted to believe Max would remain true, just

as she wanted to believe the woman *was* her mother, not her subconscious reacting to some tragic old photo or wishful thinking as her father had suggested. Either way, the shock of recognition she'd felt two weeks ago, seeing that woman, had been reinforced yesterday a thousandfold.

Ahead in the raft, Max heard her and turned around. "Wake up, Karinne."

"I'm awake."

"Not enough," he warned. "We've got Kwagunt Rapid coming up in a few miles. I don't want to fish you out again."

"I won't fall in."

"When's the next white water?" Anita asked.

"Mile 56," Max said. "But the 60s are calmer."

"Much more time to enjoy the scenery," Cory told them.

"We have to get through the rapids first," Max reminded them.

I'm beginning to hate that word, Karinne thought. The white water soon approached and despite her mood her adrenaline soared. It was hard to remain centered on anything other than the Colorado River. Max and Cory powered their way through the current, using their strong arms and shoulders to maneuver the raft. A few times Karinne thought the current might rip her paddle right out of her hand, but she held on.

She tried to think dispassionately about Max's accusation. Was there any truth to it? Karinne felt he hadn't been entirely fair. She was a successful adult, a successful professional, a responsible daughter.

But yesterday she'd fallen off the raft and panicked like a child. Karinne didn't like how the Grand Canyon put her and Max on an unequal footing, as if…as if he was her babysitter. She hated that feeling. Anywhere else they were equals. In the canyon, Max was the adult. Karinne was just along for the ride.

Were she and Max even marriage material? Had a "ghost story" ruined her wedding? Turning off her thoughts was about as easy as stopping the current, but for her own future, she'd have to discover those answers. If the next few days were as troubled as the past few, it didn't bode well.

Karinne was emotionally exhausted when the rapids finally faded into smoother water. She breathed a sigh of relief, then of enjoyment at the beauty and calmness surrounding them. Around the raft, the coarse brown Tapeats Sandstone embraced the river and rose high. Water weathered everything, even rock.

Would *she* be able to weather this latest turn of events? Karinne wanted to wear that sweatshirt, see what happened. She could put her paddle in the water and determine her own course...or would she sit and drift aimlessly like the child Max accused her of being, letting others care for her.

I can't. I won't.

"How's everyone doing?" Max asked.

"Great." Anita squeezed water out of her long braid. "Wet."

"How about you, Karinne?" Max asked.

"I could go for a breather. What's next?"

"An easy ride along calm shoreline," Max said. "We're coming up on the Little Colorado River."

"Can we get out?"

"Not yet. Park rules forbid it for another three miles," Max said. "The shores here are sacred ground to the local Hopi."

"Why?"

"The area's full of salt deposits. They're used in Native

American religious ceremonies." Max pointed to the pure-white bands that ran parallel and just above the water.

"Salt is…sacred?" Anita asked.

"The Hopi, Pueblo and Navajo harvest salt and use it in rituals," Max said. "The Zunis consider it the actual flesh of the deity."

"It's used in rituals with children," Cory added. "They believe salt nourishes life."

Karinne felt a pang inside. She imagined happy mothers with smiling babies, observing all the rites of passage in their young lives. For all but six years of her life, she hadn't experienced that with her own mother. It had been her father and the Hunters who'd been there. It had been Max at all the important events in her life. And now Max said it was over. He and Karinne would never have any children. Although Karinne had never felt a strong pull toward motherhood, that reality suddenly knifed through her.

"I'm surprised there's any salt left," Anita observed. "I thought the explorers used it to preserve food."

"Europeans weren't allowed here. According to the Zunis, not everyone was respectful of Salt Woman. That made her so angry, she left the Grand Canyon forever," Cory said.

Like my mother left us for the desert river and a fake grave?

"The deity moved to Zuni Salt Lake in western New Mexico. But at the last moment, Salt Woman relented and left some of her precious body—the deposits—behind for her people, their children and their children's children."

The mist seemed to settle in more heavily on the shore.

"It feels special here…" Anita murmured in a hushed, respectful voice.

The mist swirled above the sacred grounds Salt Woman had abandoned so long ago. Karinne could practically hear the whispers of the past in the fog, see the images that were alive, yet not alive, almost supernatural. The aura seemed to bounce off the walls with a power that pressed at her, demanding her attention. She shivered visibly.

Max noticed. He always noticed. "You want my jacket?" he asked.

"Thanks, but I have something." *It's now or never.*

Karinne laid her paddle over her lap and opened the side of her backpack. She'd packed nothing in that pocket except for the sweatshirt wrapped in a plastic bag.

"Think about what you're doing," Max said as he saw the pink. Karinne seemed to hear the child from her past warning her, as well.

"We'll stop after the salt deposits," Cory was saying. "You'll have time to warm up then."

"Karinne…are you sure about this?" Max demanded.

She nodded. *I have to know. What happened to my mother?* "You said you'd help me, Max."

Max stripped off his windbreaker and held it out to Karinne. "Last chance." She shook her head.

Karinne pulled out the plastic bag with one hand and set down the paddle.

Karinne withdrew the sweatshirt. She shed her slicker and stared at the material. The neon-pink color clashed with the pureness of the shimmering salt around them. Karinne ran her fingers along one sleeve, remembering how her mother's favorite roses were pink.

I don't know how or why, but I feel as if Mom's back.

By now Anita and Cory were watching. All conversation in the raft ceased. Cory's paddling grew noticeably faster, while Anita pretended to take in the scenery. Max's eyes grew as dark as the shadows in the rock. It didn't matter. Karinne slipped her arms inside the pink sleeves and pulled the shirt on over her head.

I have to learn the truth.

ied to take in the scene/y. Max's eyes

Chapter Seven

Anita spoke first. "It looks nice, Karinne," she said politely.

"Do you know what you're doing?" Cory asked with customary bluntness.

"Calm down, Cory," Karinne said. "Let's not fight over my wardrobe."

"This isn't about your taste in clothing!" Cory yelled. "It's about thinking things through. This person is sick. Take it off, Karinne. This could be…risky."

"Leave her alone," Max said curtly. "She wants to know. Frankly, so do I."

"You do?" Cory sounded surprised.

Karinne smiled. Max understood. It was one of the reasons she loved him.

"It's safer for Karinne to meet her mother—if she's alive—around us," Max continued, speaking to Cory. "God forbid she should run into this person alone. I promised Karinne I'd help her."

Karinne held her breath, hoping Max wouldn't add what else he'd said—that they were through. Karinne's smile faded. His offer to search for her mother had only reinforced her protected status.

"You don't need to drag Cory and Anita into this, Max."

"There's safety in numbers."

Karinne couldn't argue with that. She crossed her arms, feeling chilled, despite the dryness of the new sweatshirt. "I don't want to talk about it. Can't we just enjoy the scenery?"

"Sure." Max made a big show of steering them around a tame-looking rock formation in the middle of the river. "We're headed toward the Great Unconformity."

"I still think you're crazy, Karinne," Cory announced tersely.

"What's the Great Unconformity?" Anita asked, making an effort at conversation.

"The foundation is badly off center. Look at the tilt. It's missing a chronological order of rock," Max said.

"A big chunk of my history is missing, too," Karinne said. *Everything* seemed to remind her of that.

"I thought you didn't want to talk about it," Cory snapped.

"I don't, but I want you to understand. I refuse to have my future—mine and Max's—" she said this deliberately "—threatened. And that means finding out who sent me this top." Karinne thought of "The Toll," the skeleton in the photo. "I want more than a few notes or a piece of clothing. I want more than bare bones."

"No matter what you uncover?" Cory asked. "Even if it's some crazy person?"

"Leave it be," Max said. "She's made her decision."

Cory swore and dropped his paddle. Max retrieved it.

"Break time." Max grabbed for the waterproof map. "We can plan to have our lunch stop at the Cardenas Creek ruins eight miles downriver from here. It's the last area before more rapids, and I won't put this raft in them until everyone calms down and has his or her mind on business. I don't need any more people overboard."

No one argued.

The sun shone high overhead as the men beached and secured the raft. They all hiked up a small ridge, where the ruins were located. Max led the way, followed by Karinne, Anita and Cory. It didn't take them long to reach the tall ruins, where they sat down for lunch. Below, the river meandered through a wide area with shorelines.

"It's so open. What a great view of the canyon." Anita briskly unwrapped one of the sandwiches they'd made the night before, since no one else seemed to have an appetite. "No wonder the Pueblo Natives built the watchtower here."

Cory gestured toward the carefully fitted rocks, which had stood the test of time and thrust upward to the azure-blue of the sky. "The Colorado stays clear of white water for another sixteen miles or so."

"It'll be smooth sailing. Tomorrow, we'll be on the river and then hit Phantom Ranch again. We'll spend the night at the lodge," Max said.

"Ah, civilization." Anita sighed extravagantly. "Telephones, gift stores and running water."

"Don't forget easy access for creeps," Cory added, glaring at the pink sweatshirt.

"I want to see the watchtower ruins up close. Come on, Cory," Anita said. "Bring our food."

Cory stood and followed Anita. Karinne scanned the ruins, silently reading the guide signs. The atmosphere was tense and uneasy until Max finally spoke. "Can I ask you a hypothetical question?"

"Of course."

"If Margot wasn't the loving mother you always thought she was, would you want to know?"

"Yes," Karinne said immediately.

"Even though you were happy with her memories?"

"Max, where's this going? What's your point?"

Max gazed out into the beauty before them. The serenity of the canyon and its soaring towers and sides of rock were decidedly at odds with his expression.

"For starters, your mystery woman did more than just call a few months ago. She wanted money, supposedly to pay for her trip to come and see you. Of course I didn't give her any or make any arrangements to contact her in the future."

Karinne felt her hopes dash. "Why didn't you tell me?"

"I'm telling you now. There's something else. I called your father."

"You called Dad instead of me? Max, how could you? Why didn't you talk to me first?"

"I could ask the same thing. You should've talked to me about your mother before you talked to Cory."

Karinne flushed. "It's not the same thing. I'm not a little girl. I don't need you running to my father."

"I tried to reach you." His tone of voice accused her. "You're never at home, Karinne. Nor do you answer your cell phone."

"I can't while I'm working! You know I return your calls as soon as I can, but you're never topside when I do. It's not my fault cells don't work in the canyon."

"Nothing like a long-distance relationship without even phone contact," he said with more than a trace of bitterness. "Anyway, I called your father and talked to him. He asked me to wait until after the wedding to tell you. He's absolutely convinced that your mother's dead. I had him hire me a private detective in Phoenix. Financially, you could be taken advantage of—emotionally, as well."

"Why? Because I'm a helpless female?" she asked sharply.

Max shrugged. "Under the circumstances…"

"You decided to keep me out of the loop." Karinne's lips thinned. "Who else did you talk to? Cory?"

"He knows about the calls and the detective. And…that I saw your mother the day she disappeared." Max met her gaze.

"You *saw* her?" she echoed.

"Yes. Margot came to the house. She wanted to know where you were."

"Mom was there?"

"I told her I didn't know where you were. But I did. You were inside the house with Cory."

"Oh, my God. You lied to her?"

"I lied."

"Maybe she wanted to say goodbye." Karinne's voice shook. "I always knew she loved me…"

"Maybe she wanted to kidnap you, assuming she's alive. Or maybe she wanted to kill herself *and* you."

"Mom would never do that!"

"It's not unheard of among unhappy parents," Max said. "How do you know? Would you have guessed she'd leave a suicide note and disappear into the river?"

"Perhaps seeing me might have…might have chased away her depression. You were just a boy, Max. You had no right to make that decision."

"I did, and I can't change it. Nor would I if I had to do it over again. You didn't see Margot that day. I did. She scared me, Karinne. She wasn't herself."

Tears started down Karinne's cheeks. "And I never saw her again."

"I'm sorry."

"You should've called me! You had no right to interfere, Max."

"Whether I did or didn't makes no difference now. And

once this investigation of ours is over, I'm done interfering—or whatever you want to call it."

Karinne rubbed her eyes, then abruptly dropped her hands. "You're really serious about us breaking up?"

"What's to break up? We're never together. And as you yourself pointed out, we can't talk on the phone. Are we supposed to write each other letters every weekend and get older and lonelier as the years go by? We're not kids anymore, living on the same street. We're adults, Karinne."

"But we love each other! How can you throw it all away? I've loved you since I was a girl."

"Maybe that's the problem. I'm just a habit, a familiar routine. And you take advantage of it. Maybe I have, too. But this thing with your mother has opened my eyes. If it isn't your job, or your father, or your ghost of a mother keeping us apart, it'll be something else...some other excuse."

"But—"

Max held up his hand. "I'm not saying your reasons aren't important to you."

"No. You're just saying *I'm* not important anymore. That you're not going to wait for me."

"You're only half right. You'll always be important to me, Karinne. But let me spell it out. You want to search for a ghost? Fine. I'll even help. But I'm done waiting for a reluctant bride. You want to embrace phantoms instead of a living man, go ahead. I'd rather deal with reality, and get on with my life."

Karinne rose to her feet and turned her back on him. Max watched her leave and then hurry down to the trail to the shoreline. The most beautiful geological formation in the world spread out its rocky rainbows before them, but right now neither of them could appreciate it. After a moment, Max carefully put away the sandwiches. He signaled to Cory and Anita and, feeling as old as the rocks in the canyon, started down the trail himself.

They set up camp late in the afternoon, everyone damp and exhausted from the rapids. The two tents were set far enough apart for privacy, but for once Karinne wasn't looking forward joyfully to her and Max's time alone. Dinner had been a strained affair. Cory and Anita had obviously enjoyed each other's company, laughing, talking and planning a future, while Karinne inwardly writhed, comparing them with Max and her.

Later, after the dishes were done and the sleeping bags rolled out, Cory and Anita sat around the campfire, side by side, arms around each other with an intimacy that brought tears to her eyes. Max took off to check on the raft and the cargo that had remained stowed, leaving Karinne alone. The sounds of the river water seemed harsh, intrusive, while the darkness of the night seemed to emphasize her loneliness.

Finally she said good-night to Cory and Anita and headed for her tent, where she kicked off her boots, then lay down, fully clothed, on top of the sleeping bag. She crossed her arms behind her head and gazed upward, her eyes unfocused, remembering the past. Memories of her mother and father and happier times flooded her mind. And sharing all those memories were Cory and Max... especially Max.

She never would've guessed that Max had sent Margot away from his house without telling her. She angrily wondered why he'd kept that secret from her for so long. Her anger rose at his betrayal now in calling off their wedding. Had she really been as selfish as he thought? She didn't think so. Max and Cory had each other growing up; they still had each other as adults. As an only child, she'd clung to her mother as all little girls did, and mourned Margot's absence in her life. How could she not follow up on this mystery? And how could she make him see that loving Margot didn't detract one bit from her loving him? She'd been blessed to have Max in her life. She wasn't about to give him up without a fight.

It was past ten, late for river trips, when Max finally entered the tent. He saw Karinne, still dressed, awake.

"We have an early day tomorrow. You should get to bed," he suggested, sitting on his own bag and untying his sneakers.

"Kind of hard to sleep," she responded. "You dumped me today, remember?"

Max said nothing. She sat up and crossed her legs, watching him undress. She took in the strength of his shoulders, the hard chest she'd snuggled up to so many times, the lean hips. He stripped down to his briefs, hesitated, removed those and climbed into his sleeping bag, leaving the side unzipped. Like Karinne, though, he remained sitting.

"Do you want to talk about it?" she asked.

"No."

"Then we won't talk. We'll make love instead." Karinne started to undress.

"Karinne..."

"Your exact words were...when this business with your mother is over, we're done. It's not over yet. No reason we can't enjoy each other's company." She dropped her shirt, and then her jeans. "I still love you. It's been a long time since we've been together. You can't say you haven't missed me."

"You're just making things harder," Max said, but he didn't look away as she dropped her bra and panties onto the pile of discarded clothing.

"One last time, Max," she said, kneeling before him. "One last time, and I won't ask again."

For a moment she thought he'd rebuff her, but he didn't. He reached for her and brought her close, his lips meeting hers. Then he pulled her down and stroked the bare skin of her back, murmuring words of love. She responded the way she always did with him, her body and soul drinking him in, her heart throbbing with the joy and passion he aroused in her. But this time, their physical satisfaction left her emotionally unfulfilled.

And later, when Karinne crawled back into her own sleeping bag, Max didn't protest. It was only then that she realized Max could be right. Perhaps it was truly over, after all.

But then she heard Max say, "Karinne?"

She forced herself to answer calmly. "Yes?"

"I wanted you to see how I live. Really live, not just on weekends. That's why I wanted this trip. I needed to know if you could love this place, too, enough to be here with me."

Hope welled within her. "Then let me try. I've made mistakes. You're right about my father," she admitted. "He does need more than I can give him."

Silence.

"I shouldn't have expected you to raise our family alone," Max admitted.

Karinne almost smiled. "Well, we're making progress. Max, don't write us off yet."

"No," he said simply. "But if by some miracle things go well—and I'm not making any promises—can you live without your career?" he asked.

"It'd be hard. I'll always be a photographer." She paused, then asked a more difficult question in return. "Do you think you could give up having children? Could you be happy with it just being us?"

"It'd be hard," he echoed. "Especially if you intend to go chasing after your mother."

"Even if she's alive?"

"I know you, Karinne. You'll want to make up lost years if she is."

Karinne couldn't deny it.

"No matter what happens, you'll have to choose between your parents and me," Max said finally. "If that's too much for you, then when this trip is over, you accept that we're done. We'll be civilized adults, okay?"

Karinne thought of the unsatisfactory lovemaking they'd just shared. Max was right. They couldn't live the rest of their lives this way.

"Okay."

THE NEXT MORNING dawned clear and sunny, but Karinne had no heart for the beauty of the day, the canyon or the river. Nor did she have any enthusiasm for the three sets of rapids the raft entered once they left Cardenas Creek. She felt physically dull and emotionally heartbroken, so much so that Cory spoke to her once they got to Mile 77, start of the Upper Granite Gorge.

"Karinne, what's wrong?" he asked.

She pushed her wet, straggling hair out of her face. "I didn't sleep well last night." In her peripheral vision she saw Max lift his head sharply, but couldn't meet his gaze. She determinedly studied the pink of the mica and the milky white of the quartz, crystallized Precambrian rock glistening in the sun.

"Wake up," Max said harshly. "These gorge walls narrow substantially. They'll constrict the river and drastically speed up the current. We'll be hitting three sets of rapids with very little breathing space all the way to Phantom Ranch."

"How little breathing space?" Anita asked.

"Two sets of rapids before we clear Creek Canyon at mile 84, then another set before we reach the Kaibab Trail."

Unaccountably, Karinne felt like bursting into tears. Instead, she concentrated on keeping herself safe and managed to control her emotions. By the end of the longest day of her life, they finally got to Phantom Ranch. Karinne was relieved when Cory checked them in at the front desk. Outside, the shadows lengthened from one canyon wall to the other and covered the rustic lodge near the north side of the river. Close to Bright Angel Creek lay a tent campground for the hardier tourists. Various watercraft were docked for the night. The mules in the corrals were already eating a well-deserved dinner. Inside, other sightseers headed for semiprivate bunking areas or the men's and women's dormitories. The brothers had secured a private cabin, which, unlike the dorms, had its own sink, toilet and bathing area.

Karinne wasn't looking forward to putting on a cheerful face with the other three in such close quarters. Max had managed to act like his usual self, but Karinne wasn't having as easy a time. How could Max throw away everything they'd shared?

Along with the grief and anguish, she felt anger. Max had no right to use Margot as a reason for ending their engagement. He could've been indirectly responsible for Margot's death, if she truly was dead. What if Margot *had* been able to see Karinne that fateful day? What if the sight of her loving daughter could have wiped out whatever dark thoughts and deeds she carried within? Max couldn't be correct about a proposed kidnapping. Margot would never take her away from her father. As for a murder-suicide, Karinne didn't believe that, either.

But she couldn't mull over these ideas, couldn't cry or

rave about them. She had to share a tiny cabin with three other people, one of them her ex-fiancé.

"At least we won't have to use the dorm's communal showers," Cory was saying. "We'll have our own bathroom."

Max accepted the old-fashioned key attached by brass to an artful piece of carved wood. "The cabins do have more privacy."

"I like the rustic feel," Karinne said, forcing herself to participate in the conversation.

"Look, a real *key* instead of a magnetic strip card," Anita marveled. "And the wood's a carved deer."

"We're room Deer-15," Cory said. "*A* is antelope, then bear, cougar, deer and so on."

"May I?" Anita asked, gesturing toward the key.

"Sure." Max tossed it to Anita to admire. She passed it to Karinne, who pocketed it in her jeans. "Our cabin has two single beds," Max was saying. "You and Karinne can have them. Cory and I can bunk on the floor."

"Unless you find room to squeeze me in." Cory grinned at Anita.

Karinne deliberately avoided Max's eyes. She doubted he'd be making any offers to snuggle in a single bed.

The four made their way through the crowds to their cabin. Cory unlocked the door and they all dropped their gear.

"We should eat first and shower later," Cory said; the others agreed.

After a quick wipe of their trail-dusty hands and faces, they hurried toward the dining area, Cory and Anita leading the way. The line waiting to eat was long; the wood-and-twine-bound chairs at wooden trestle tables provided limited seating. People smelling of sweat and bug spray were packed in as tightly as possible. But the hot stew, bread and brownies served family-style were delicious. Adults busied themselves with "chowing down." Even children, prone to laughing and talking, were eating with the single-minded hunger triggered by outdoor air and exercise.

Karinne still had half the food left on her plate when the others set down their silverware. The servings were extremely generous, she'd thought, and the others ate with relish. At least eating gave her an excuse for not talking. Max had finished first and was getting another cup of coffee. Anita had gone back in line for seconds. Karinne set her fork on the table.

"Done already?" Cory asked. "I assumed you'd be starving."

"I'm not really hungry," Karinne admitted.

"Then if you don't mind…" Cory swapped his empty plate for her half-filled one. "This way, I won't have to stand in line again."

"Speaking of lines, I think I'll go shower first. I have the room key." She was eager to escape Max and have a few minutes to herself.

"Oh. I'll walk you over," Cory said politely, reluctantly putting down his fork.

"Don't. You're not finished eating, and Max and Anita will lose the table." Karinne gestured to all the people with trays standing against the wall. "See you back at the cabin."

Cory nodded, fork in hand again as he tackled Karinne's leftover stew.

Karinne threaded her way through the crowds standing in line, indoors and out, breathing a sigh of relief as she escaped. Phantom Ranch was as busy as any convention center; people crowded the grounds, some of them eating picnic-style, while others were busy inspecting exhibits, signs and park maps. Pink sweatshirt or not, she doubted anyone, including her mother, could spot her in this mob scene.

She really wanted a shower. She reached their cabin and walked inside. She pulled off the sweatshirt, and placed it and the key on the nightstand. After a moment, she decided to leave the entrance door unlocked. She wasn't planning a long shower, but she didn't want to have to cut it short to let the others in. She gathered a fresh set of clothes, plus her wallet with ID and money, then stepped into the tiny bathroom, latched the door and stripped for a quick shower. The water was warm enough for comfort, but she wouldn't have minded another towel. Fortunately, there was a mirror. She brushed her teeth and hair, then got dressed, still in the bathroom.

She unlatched the bathroom door, rolling up her dirty laundry to stow away—and heard someone move inside the cabin.

"Is that you, Max?" she called, opening the door.

The person sitting on the bed wasn't Max but a woman. She rose and stood awkwardly, the lined face familiar, as was her voice.

"Hello, Karinne."

Karinne dropped her dirty laundry on the floor.

"Mom?"

Chapter Eight

"It's me," Margot said.

Karinne stared. *I knew it. I knew I wasn't crazy.*

Margot held out her arms. "Can I have a hug?"

Karinne didn't hesitate. She rushed into her mother's arms. The two women held each other tightly, too overwhelmed for tears or smiles. After long minutes, Margot gently released her daughter.

"Come on, sweetheart. Let's walk over to my place."

Margot had her own cabin, Bear-3, with its intricately carved wooden animal on the end of the key. They were a ten-minute walk from Karinne's, but neither noticed the passage of time.

"So I *did* see you on the pontoon," Karinne said.

"You scared me to death when you fell off the raft. I didn't mean to startle you," Margot apologized.

"And I saw you in the stadium in Phoenix, too."

"Yes."

"How long have you been here in the canyon?" Karinne asked.

"A week. I was determined to see you, even if you didn't wear my gift."

"But I did."

"The pink's very loud, isn't it? It's all the gift shop had in your size."

Karinne smiled. "Why didn't you call me or come to my apartment? Or the house? Why call Max? Why the cloak-and-dagger routine?" Then the questions she had came tumbling out. "Why didn't you come home? Where were you all this time?"

Margot's own smile faded. "It's not a story I'm proud of, but it's one you have a right to know. Let's go inside."

Margot unlocked her cabin. The two women sat side by side on one of the beds, the mother holding both of her daughter's hands as they talked.

"I had—have—a gambling problem," she said quietly. "I don't understand why, but it's always been there. My father was a gambler, too. You never knew him, Karinne, but he used to live for horse races, greyhound tracks, casinos… You name it, he bet on it. I went with him. And when I was old enough, I gambled, too. Not for fun, like a normal person. It's a disease. My disease."

"I never would've guessed, Mom."

"It's true. I hid it for years and fought to stop, but I never could for long. When I was dating your father, I realized I had to do something. I started going to Gamblers Anonymous meetings. Once we were married, I'd stopped cold turkey. I stayed that way for years. Then I had you and while I was home taking care of a child, I got bored. I missed my job, felt sorry for myself, your father was off traveling and I was stuck at home. That's no excuse—but I started gambling again."

Margot's voice grew shaky, and then she steadied herself.

"First it was just card games for pennies with the other young moms in the neighborhood. Then lotto tickets. I told myself it was okay. I wasn't betting much. But by the time you started school and I returned to work, I had the fever again. I went back to old habits and high stakes. I gambled away all my paychecks. Then I started in on your father's earnings. He found out."

"But Dad didn't leave you," Karinne said, confused.

"No. I began going back to meetings, and he took safeguards to protect our finances. But I never realized how much a child could affect our careers. We decided no more children. I stayed home with you more—and I resented you both." Margot swallowed hard. "Again, no excuse."

"Dad didn't know?"

"Not at first. I'd pretend to be working on local photography assignments while I went to the casinos. Then I made a huge win at blackjack—more money than your father and I could have earned working in a year. I told everyone I'd quit my job and taken a sabbatical. It was true—I wanted to experiment and expand my creative skills. I thought I could stay away from gambling with that big win. Your father was pleased I could take you along with me, and so was I. But eventually I started gambling again and lost all the money I'd made."

"What happened? Why the suicide note? Why did you just disappear?"

"I couldn't come home. You need to know what I did the day before." Margot clasped her hands together tightly. "I took out a new mortgage on our house—the house your father had paid off. I had a 'sure thing' at the track. And I'd already placed the largest bet I'd ever made. My past winnings, the house, my business, everything... I knew I couldn't lose. But I did."

"So you just left? And pretended to kill yourself?"

"I had to. I couldn't face either of you with the truth. Your father would've divorced me, and taken you with him. No court would give me custody. But my disappearance...what looked like my death—" Margot's voice broke "—would solve everything. My life insurance, which included suicide coverage, would save the house. You and your father could have normal lives."

"Normal?"

"I thought of you and your father every day, Karinne! Whether I came home or not, I'd lose you both. Once your father cashed my life insurance, I couldn't reverse my decision. I'd be convicted of insurance fraud, and he might've been, too. So I stayed away."

"And just decided to come back now?" Karinne asked.

"I wanted to see you. I subscribe to the local paper. When I saw you were getting married, I had to come home. The statute of limitations has expired. Karinne, when I saw you wearing that pink sweatshirt, I hoped so much. I know I haven't been the world's greatest mother, but if it's not too much to ask…"

"What?" Karinne tried to add *Mom,* but the word felt strange on her tongue.

"Can we start again?"

CORY HAD JUST cleared away Karinne's plate when Max and Anita returned to the table.

"Where's Karinne?" Anita asked.

"She went to the cabin."

"You let her go *alone?*" Max asked.

"She wanted to shower."

"You should've gone with her!" Max dropped his plate on the table and rushed off.

"Should we go, too?" Anita asked Cory.

"I don't think so. Why don't you finish eating?"

"I'll get a carton for Max's food. Why didn't you go with her, Cory?"

"Because we're surrounded by hundreds of people. Karinne'll be safe here."

"But...what about this crazy woman?"

"People have been touring the Grand Canyon since the 1880s. We get five million visitors a year. There's never been a single murder." Cory gestured toward Anita's empty seat with his fork.

Anita cast a nervous glance toward the door. "I guess Max will take care of her."

"And Karinne needs to take care of Max," Cory said firmly. "This is the very first time she's ever come to the canyon, to Max's world, for more than a weekend. This visit is long overdue. She shouldn't let some freak distract her."

"You could say the same about me. I've never been down the river before."

"No, but you've been to Grand Canyon Village lots of times. Max usually sees Karinne in Phoenix."

"Max doesn't have an elderly father, either." Anita replaced her paper napkin on her lap. "Could *you* ever leave here, Cory?"

"If I had to. If our marriage really needed it."

Anita nodded. "As close as Karinne and I are, she never talks about her mother. Is she dead or not?"

"Margot? I don't know," Cory said.

"What was she like?" Anita asked curiously.

"Max and I never liked her as kids. Margot Cavanaugh was no gem." Cory remembered. "If she's back, she wants something. It's not for any hearts-and-flowers reunion at Karinne's wedding."

KARINNE LISTENED again to her mother's request.

"Can you forgive me? I did what I thought was best."

"I—I can try. Are you coming back to Phoenix?" Karinne asked.

"No."

"Can we can stay in touch?"

"I'd like that, Karinne. I've never stopped loving you. I can't change the past, but I want to be part of your future. I don't expect a wedding invitation."

Slowly Karinne said, "I've always wanted you there, Mom. I never stopped missing you."

The desperate hope on Margot's face would have softened the hardest of hearts. "Are you inviting me?"

"If there's a wedding, yes, you'll be there."

Margot and Karinne wrapped their arms around each other.

"We have so much to catch up on," Karinne murmured when they finally broke their embrace.

"Too much," Margot said. "We'll definitely need coffee."

"We can go back to the mess hall."

Margot wiped at her eyes with a tissue. Her mascara came off in black smudges on the tissue.

"Go fix your face, and I'll call Max—let him know where I am."

Margot smiled and closed the bathroom door. Karinne picked up the phone, then thought, *I wonder what Dad will say.*

MAX STARED AT Deer-15, their empty cabin. He'd searched the room once, then twice, for a note. Although his breathing remained normal, his heart seemed to race a mile a minute. Her pile of soiled clothing lay on the floor. Karinne was a neat, organized person. *What was going on?* He felt like running out and screaming her name, but fought down the urge.

Be sensible, he told himself. *She's in the gift shop. Or you missed her in the crowd.*

Max didn't believe that for a second. His instincts told

him something unusual had happened. But what? He couldn't bear the idea of Karinne being hurt or upset. He loved her. He'd always loved her, and the sick feeling in the pit of his stomach was almost crippling as he considered his plan of action. He was debating whether to wait in the cabin or go back to Cory and Anita when the room phone rang. He snatched it up. "Hello?"

"Max, it's me."

"Karinne! Where are you?"

At first he couldn't understand the rush of words. Then he did. "Your mother's here?" he asked incredulously.

"Yes. I'm in her cabin."

"Where?"

"Bear-3."

"I'm coming over."

"Love you."

Max heard the phone disconnect as she hung up. He scribbled a note for Cory and Anita and hurried toward the Bear group of cabins. As he did, he willed his racing heart to slow down. Breaking their engagement hadn't changed his feelings for her. He'd fallen in love with her during her high school graduation, when he'd sat watching with her family and his. He'd been four years older and later tried to convince himself that his fondness for Karinne was a sentimental reaction to the ceremony, but he knew better.

Karinne had left to go to college, and during those four years he'd continued in his role as family friend. Cory, who was closer to Karinne's age and attending the same college, kept him posted on her, and of course Max saw her from time to time. It wasn't until after her college graduation that Karinne had miraculously admitted that she felt the same way he did way back in her high school days, but had been too young and too shy to admit it. They'd grown close, then became lovers, then got engaged. But the engagement had dragged on and on and on as Karinne established herself in her new career.

By this time Max had his own career, but for Karinne, he'd offered to find something new. Arizona was the land of the great outdoors, and for a man like him, there were always opportunities. Karinne hadn't felt he should leave his job in the Grand Canyon. Now that he employed Cory, it was too late for him to quit without damaging his brother's finances, and now Cory was married.

Max had waited years for Karinne to finish school. Then he'd waited for her to follow her dreams—although he wondered if sports photography was Jeff Cavanaugh's dream pushed onto his daughter instead of Karinne's true dream. Nonetheless, he'd waited. And waited. Max was an all or nothing kind of person. But Karinne seemed content with the small parts of him she had time for, while Max wanted a wife, children, a life. Karinne wanted to live in the past or drift in the present, never planning for a future. It wasn't enough. He couldn't do it anymore. But that didn't mean he could just dismiss her. Just the hint of any risk to her tightened his chest with worry.

He reached the cabin. His knock on the door was loud and brisk. To Max's immense relief, Karinne herself answered.

"That was fast," she said, glowing. "Come say hello to my mother."

Max immediately recognized her, not just from memory but her resemblance to Karinne. Despite the age difference, they shared the same body type, the same face. Only where Karinne's mouth was generous and smiling, Margot's thin lips moved nervously.

"Hello, Max," Margot said with a shy smile. "It's been a long time."

"Yes, it has." The old words from the past sprang to his lips. "Welcome back, Mrs. C."

"It's Margot, please. You've grown tall. And strong." She extended her hand to Max.

He took it briefly. "I've been rafting."

"Max, I want to bow out of the rest of the trip," Karinne said apologetically, with a significant glance toward her mother. "I'd like to stay here alone with Mom."

He bit back the words. *Over my dead body.*

"No, you don't have to do that. You should stick to your original arrangements," Margot said.

Margot doesn't want to be with her own daughter? After all this time? He maintained his silence.

"But, Mom, you just got here!" Karinne protested.

"I'll still be here when you get back from rafting, Karinne."

Karinne's face clearly said, *Will you?*

Max sighed. "Perhaps your mother would like to join us tomorrow on the river," he suggested. There was no way he'd leave Karinne alone with Margot. Max wasn't buying the perfect-mother routine for a second. Where had she been all these years?

"If you don't mind, Karinne…then thank you, Max. That sounds lovely," Margot agreed, almost too quickly. "I should go shopping. I have to pick up some things if I'm going rafting."

"I'll come with you," Karinne insisted.

"It's okay, darling," Margot said. "I'll get an early night and see you tomorrow."

"But…I thought we could spend more time together!"

"Tomorrow, sweetheart."

Margot practically forced her daughter out of the room. Karinne looked to Max for help but, when none was forthcoming, reluctantly hugged and kissed her mother goodbye.

Margot backed into the cabin as Karinne stepped out.

Max grabbed the door handle, putting himself between Margot, who was inside, and Karinne outside. "We'll leave after the first breakfast, Mrs. Cavanaugh."

"Won't you call me Margot? We should be friends," Margot urged.

Max remembered how he'd lied to Margot as a boy. He doubted Margot had ever realized that.

"As long as Karinne's happy, Margot, that won't be a problem. I have to wonder, though…"

"What?"

"What do you *really* want?" Max asked the older woman.

Margot smiled, but the smile didn't reach her eyes. "The same as you. I want Karinne."

Chapter Nine

Max walked hand in hand with Karinne back to their cabin.

"Mom and I barely got to speak to each other. It was almost as if…she couldn't wait to get rid of me," Karinne said slowly.

"Maybe she was just overwhelmed," Max suggested.

"After all these years, she finally shows up, and all I get is a few minutes?"

"You sound a bit overwhelmed yourself." He squeezed her hand. "Don't worry. Once she's on the raft she'll be a captive audience."

"There is that." Karinne smiled. "Thank you for inviting her, Max."

"So…what did she have to say? Anything you want to share?"

Karinne related her mother's tale. At the end of it, Max shook his head.

"Sad, isn't it?"

Karinne nodded. "And I still have to call Dad."

"That's one conversation he won't be expecting. Do you think he's up to hearing it?"

"I hope so. I don't want to upset him too much. Still, he has to be told."

They arrived at their own cabin, but instead of going in, Karinne lingered on the porch steps outside the cabin.

"I invited Mom to the wedding," she said. "It…kind of slipped out. Do you mind?"

"Karinne, I told you," he said softly, "there isn't going to be any wedding."

"But you thought I was chasing ghosts. I wasn't, Max! Mom's alive!"

"That doesn't change things."

"You're right. It doesn't change things for me. I'm marrying you, come hell or high water. And I'd like Mom to be there."

Max started to argue, then didn't. Karinne had just had a major shock. He wasn't going to add to it, although he'd meant what he said. "Did Margot say yes?"

"Not exactly."

"Talk about Margot all you want, but don't say anything about yet another wedding that won't happen," Max said curtly, ignoring the way she blanched. "Why don't you go on in and use the phone? I'll wait out here until you're done, if you want."

Karinne nodded. She unlocked the cabin door, and tossed him the key. "I won't be long."

Karinne settled herself on the bed and dialed her old home number. Jeff answered on the third ring.

"Hi, Dad, it's me."

"Karinne? I didn't expect to hear from you, of all people! I thought you were rafting."

"I was. I am. We're at Phantom Ranch. I don't know how to tell you this, so I'll just come out and say it. Mom's alive, and she's here. A few cabins away."

The silence on the other end screamed with tension.

"Are you sure?" Jeff finally asked, his voice hoarse.

"It's her, Dad. Mom's alive."

Another pause, then, "What does she have to say for herself? Did she bother explaining where she's been all these years?"

"Dad, I don't want to upset you. Your heart…"

"I'll be more upset if you don't tell me," Jeff said, his voice sounding more normal. "What did she say, Karinne?"

She related everything Margot had said, concluding with, "I just finished seeing her. She's supposed to go rafting with us tomorrow."

"Your mother turns up out of nowhere and decides it's time to cruise down the Colorado? She's got a hell of a lot of nerve!" Jeff protested.

"I thought we could get reacquainted. Max invited her."

Jeff swore. "Is Max there?"

"Yes, but—"

"Let me speak to him."

Karinne put her hand over the mouthpiece. "Max? Dad wants to talk to you."

Max hurried in and Karinne handed him the phone. She couldn't hear what her father said, but the conversation was short.

"No, don't do anything," Max said. "You take care of yourself. Yeah, I will. Goodbye."

"He hung up?" Karinne asked incredulously.

"Yes. He said to tell you he feels fine, and not to cut your visit short on his account."

"But he didn't say— He didn't make arrangements to see Mom."

"With his health, I'd let the news sink in."

"I'll call him back tonight and check on him. And maybe you can have your parents drop in on him," Karinne said.

"I'll call them right now." Max was as good as his

word. His mother said she'd look in on Jeff. "And I should touch base with the private investigator, too," Max told Karinne.

"Max, I'll be outside. I need some fresh air."

"Fine. I'll come get you when I'm done." Parker Investigations had been thorough and, while expressing surprise at Margot's present location, had information of their own to impart.

"She's been living in Mexico all this time?" Max asked.

"Yes, in Baja. She hasn't done any photography work under her former name *or* her new one, Margaret Lazar. There's a man in the picture, but I haven't found much else yet."

"How's she supporting herself?"

"She started out as a waitress in a bar, then switched over to working casinos. She watches the security cameras for cheaters. I haven't filled in the rest of the gaps yet."

"Did you check to see if she's gambling—run up debts?"

"There aren't any that I can find. Nor have I found any criminal record of her in Mexico. I'm still working on any personal contacts she might have—family, friends. I have her home address."

"What about the insurance fraud implications? Can she still be held liable in the state of Arizona?"

"Not in a criminal court. The statute of limitations has expired. I suppose the insurance company could file a civil lawsuit for damages if they knew she was alive and back in the country. Since they don't…she seems to be off the hook for now."

"Thanks," Max said. "Stay on it. I don't want my—" *ex-fiancée?* "—Karinne or Jeff Cavanaugh burned by Margot. I'll call back in a few days." As he hung up, he saw Karinne, who had caught the last of the conversation, reenter the cabin.

"That was a lousy thing to say about my mother."

"She's already asked me for money once. What's to prevent her from asking you or your father?"

"She wouldn't!"

Max lifted an eyebrow in disbelief.

"Well, if she did, she'd have to have a good reason. And speaking of money, Max, why not discharge the investigator? Why pay good money when we have Mom right here?"

"Because we have too many unanswered questions. Has Margot given you her address? Phone number? Or any way to contact her?"

"Not yet, but she said she wants to stay in touch with me."

"Has she told you where she's been living all these years? Or with whom? Has she even wanted to spend a few hours with you catching up?"

"No…"

"Margot isn't exactly known for her truthfulness," Max said. "I don't trust her, and you shouldn't, either. Until we learn more, I'd feel better with a professional on our side."

"I don't need a private eye to get me Mom's address. I can get it myself." Karinne defiantly reached for the phone. "And if she's not at her cabin, I'll find her. I'm not going to lose her again."

Max reached for her arm. "Karinne, the detective got her Mexican address. You can have that. And if he obtains a local address, as well, I'll make sure you get that, too."

Max didn't add that the detective had come up with another startling piece of information. Medical records showed that Margot had taken maternity leave from her casino ten years ago. The detective hadn't received the actual birth certificate yet, but according to his research, Margot had another child with the last name of Lazar. Karinne had a sibling.

She hung up the phone without calling. "This is all so confusing. I have a million questions and no answers. Why doesn't she want to see me until tomorrow? She's been watching me for weeks, maybe months, and I haven't seen hide nor hair of her until now."

Max gathered her into his arms. He couldn't help it. "I don't think Margot would have come all this way just to disappear again after a few hours. If you really want, we can walk back over there."

"No, she doesn't want me at her cabin," Karinne said as he hugged her closer. "I've waited all these years," she said with resignation. "I guess I can wait another day."

"That's the spirit. For a moment, I thought you might camp out on her porch."

"Now, why would I want to do that when I have a whole night free to spend with you?"

Max slowly let his arms drop. "There are four of us in the cabin and only two twin beds, remember? I'll be sleeping on the floor."

"If Cory and Anita weren't in the room, we could push the twin beds together," Karinne said. "I know you still love me," she added.

"That was never the question, Karinne. But sometimes love isn't enough."

"How can you say that?"

"Margot loved you. She says she still does. But it didn't keep the two of you together, did it?"

"So Mom shows up and you disappear? Just like that?"

"Not until this trip is over. Not until we find out what's going on with Margot. I promised you that much."

Karinne lifted her hands, resting them on his broad shoulders. "Then promise me this, too. Promise you'll give me that same amount of time to try to win you back."

She wasn't rewarded with a smile, but a single, curt nod. For now, it was enough.

Send For
2 FREE BOOKS
Today!

I accept your offer!

Please send me two free
Harlequin American Romance®
novels and two mystery
gifts (gifts worth about $10).
I understand that these books
are completely free—even
the shipping and handling will
be paid—and I am under no
obligation to purchase anything, ever,
as explained on the back of this card.

**About how many NEW paperback fiction books have you
purchased in the past 3 months?**

❏ 0-2   ❏ 3-6   ❏ 7 or more
E9TY   **E9UC**   **E9UN**

154/354 HDL

Please Print

FIRST NAME

LAST NAME

ADDRESS

APT.#   CITY

STATE/PROV.   ZIP/POSTAL CODE

*Visit us online at
www.ReaderService.com*

Offer limited to one per household and not applicable to series that subscriber is currently receiving.

Your Privacy—The Reader Service is committed to protecting your privacy. Our Privacy Policy is available online at www.ReaderService.com or upon request from the Reader Service. We make a portion of our mailing list available to reputable third parties that offer products we believe may interest you. If you prefer that we not exchange your name with third parties, or if you wish to clarify or modify your communication preferences, please visit us at www.ReaderService.com/consumerschoice or write to us at Reader Service Preference Service, P.O. Box 9062, Buffalo, NY 14269. Include your complete name and address.

© 2010 HARLEQUIN ENTERPRISES LIMITED. ® and ™ are trademarks owned and used by the trademark owner and/or its licensee. Printed in the U.S.A. ▲ Detach card and mail today. No stamp needed. ▲ H-AR-03/11

The Reader Service—Here's how it works: Accepting your 2 free books and 2 free gifts (gifts valued at approximately $10.00) places you under no obligation to buy anything. You may keep the books and gifts and return the shipping statement marked "cancel." If you do not cancel, about a month later we'll send you 4 additional books and bill you just $4.24 each in the U.S. or $4.99 each in Canada. That is a savings of 15% off the cover price. It's quite a bargain! Shipping and handling is just 50¢ per book in the U.S. and 75¢ per book in Canada.* You may cancel at any time, but if you choose to continue, every month we'll send you 4 more books, which you may either purchase at the discount price or return to us and cancel your subscription.

*Terms and prices subject to change without notice. Prices do not include applicable taxes. Sales tax applicable in N.Y. Canadian residents will be charged applicable taxes. Offer not valid in Quebec. Credit or debit balances in a customer's account(s) may be offset by any other outstanding balance owed by or to the customer. Please allow 4 to 6 weeks for delivery. Offer available while quantities last. All orders subject to credit approval. Books received may not be as shown.

▼ If offer card is missing write to: The Reader Service, P.O. Box 1867, Buffalo, NY 14240-1867 or visit www.ReaderService.com ▼

NO POSTAGE
NECESSARY
IF MAILED
IN THE
UNITED STATES

BUSINESS REPLY MAIL
FIRST-CLASS MAIL   PERMIT NO. 717   BUFFALO, NY

POSTAGE WILL BE PAID BY ADDRESSEE

THE READER SERVICE
PO BOX 1867
BUFFALO NY 14240-9952

Chapter Ten

"Mom's back" was her first waking thought. "I need to get Max to marry me" was her second.

Karinne opened her eyes, confused yet rested. She tossed away her covers, fully expecting to be the first one out of bed. But Cory and Anita were already gone, and Max was dressed. He put away the map he'd been studying.

"Good morning," he said.

"Why didn't you wake me?"

"I tried. You were out cold."

She rubbed her eyes and, from a sitting position, looked around. "Where is everyone?"

"Cory and Anita went to get in line for breakfast. Your mother's joining us."

Karinne scrambled for clean clothes and dressed hurriedly. She noticed that the other packs were still in the room.

"Aren't we checking out?"

"Later, or we'll miss first breakfast. The sun hasn't reached us yet—you might want to grab a jacket. Ready?" he asked.

"Oh, yes." Karinne leaned forward to give him an enthusiastic hug and good-morning kiss. Max responded enough to put a smile on her face. Yesterday had been traumatic, but that was yesterday. Today, she had her mother back, Max

in her arms and a fresh start with both of them. Despite the
shadows on the canyon floor, the sun far above seemed to
shine particularly bright and the air seemed extraordinarily
clear as she and Max joined the others. Cory and Anita had
brought trays of food for them and secured seats. Margot
was at their table.

"Good morning, everyone. Mom…" Karinne hugged
her mother and sat down next to her.

"I'm here, darling. I'm not going anywhere."

Anita made a special effort to converse with Margot,
Karinne saw. Max seemed somewhat reserved, as did Cory,
only interacting when Margot spoke directly to them. The
brothers didn't seem very pleased about Margot's resurrec-
tion, although neither made any remarks that would detract
from Karinne's happiness.

"Are you sure you don't mind me rafting with you?"
Margot asked Max. "I know Karinne said you have the
room and the supplies, but if it's any inconvenience…"

"Glad to have you along," Max replied briskly.

"Yes," Anita seconded. "What better way for us all to
become, uh, reacquainted with the mother of the bride?"

Karinne held her breath but Max nodded his agreement without mentioning that their engagement was on
rocky ground, and Margot visibly relaxed. The topic of the
wedding remained the subject of conversation throughout
breakfast. Max didn't participate, and Karinne hoped it
meant he was reconsidering his stance.

"I wish I could see your engagement ring," Margot
said.

"I left it at home. Didn't want to risk losing it," Karinne
replied.

"I want details! And tell me about your dress, the church,
the reception…and who's coming."

"You are, of course," Karinne insisted.

"If I did, I wouldn't take any attention away from you and Max, I promise," Margot said.

"I'm sure everyone would be happy to have you there, Mom."

"Your father might not agree…" Margot's voice drifted off uneasily. "But never mind. I promised myself today would be all about good things, nothing negative. Now, tell me about the cake."

"White icing, silver edging and cut flowers. It's five tiers, white alternating with chocolate," Karinne explained. "I've had it picked out for ages, but I haven't ordered it yet."

"You didn't tell me that!" Anita said.

"Chocolate cake?" echoed Margot.

"Why not? Max and I love chocolate, but the whole thing is covered in white icing. The centerpiece will match the flower arrangements…. I've had the wedding scheduled twice before, but now I'm so glad I have it booked for November. You'll be there!"

MAX BIT HIS TONGUE as he listened to the discussion, his patience tested to the limit. All the time they'd been together, Karinne had never shown such possessiveness. Now that they weren't engaged anymore—not as far as he was concerned, anyway—she was suddenly the passionate romantic. Karinne wasn't taking him seriously. Nor was she reacting to her mother's reappearance with an ounce of sense. Instead of questioning Margot, she was playing eager bride to a loving parent. Only Karinne wasn't going to be a bride, and Margot wasn't much of a parent. Still, the last thing he wanted to do was embarrass Karinne in front of the others or ruin her joy in the reunion.

"Where are you going to stay in Phoenix?" Karinne asked, pouring her mother another cup of coffee.

"Probably a little motel," Margot said.

"No, let me pay for a nice hotel. Or maybe you could stay with Dad until the wedding."

Max hid his dismay at Karinne's suggestion. Cory actually rolled his eyes. Karinne had a big heart, but she needed more tact. He wondered if Karinne's father would be as forgiving. Fortunately, Margot had the same idea.

"Unless that invitation comes from your father, I'd better not," Margot said carefully. "Although I'd like to see Jeff again. And Phoenix."

"Then stay with me and Anita," Karinne offered.

"That's very generous of you," Margot said, smiling.

Cory threw Max a telling glance. Obviously he didn't want Margot staying with Anita—not until they knew more about her. However, Max had background information from the investigator that no one else possessed. He intended to make use of it right now, to see how honest Margot would be.

"So…where've you been living?" Max asked, lightly salting his eggs.

"Mexico, mostly."

"Are you still taking photographs?" Cory asked, passing Max the pepper.

"I never stopped, but I've been focusing on children's portraits in my spare time. Karinne, you've turned into a great photographer. I have a scrapbook of some of your sports photos, darling. I've kept it all these years." She paused. "What would you like as a wedding gift, by the way?"

"You coming home is the only gift I need." Karinne smiled.

"How long *are* you staying?" Cory asked bluntly, saving Max the question.

"Not long. I'll come back for the wedding. I can't take too much time off work."

Max could well believe that. Margot couldn't be doing well financially, or she wouldn't have asked him for money when she'd called.

"Where are you working, Mom? Out of the house or a studio?"

Max waited for Margot to lie, but she didn't.

"Neither. I work full-time, screening security monitors at a casino. It's not as interesting as photography, but it does require a good eye, which I have."

Margot certainly was a charmer, he had to admit. Karinne and Margot and even Anita were chatting like any normal family and friends. Cory joined in the conversation as needed, but like Max, he'd cooled off after Karinne offered to take Margot into his wife's apartment before the wedding. The instincts that kept both brothers alive on the river had kicked into overdrive. Margot Cavanaugh, alias Margaret Lazar, might love her daughter, but her definition of love wasn't exactly orthodox. Karinne was glowing, so Max would bide his time, vowing to keep a close eye on both mother and daughter.

At least he'd have help. He'd filled Cory in on most of the information from the detective, including Margot's alias.

The first breakfast was almost finished. Soon the canteen hall would be cleared to make way for the second. They had ten minutes before they had to leave. Cory popped a piece of toast crust into his mouth. Anita slugged down the last of her cooled coffee.

"Mom, we need to pick up our packs," Karinne said. "Where's yours?"

"In my cabin."

"You're still rafting with us, right?" Cory asked.

Margot hesitated. "I was thinking...maybe I should've mentioned it before. I, um, have a roommate," she murmured. "He'd like to come along."

"Oh," Karinne said. "I didn't see anyone last night."

Max's eyes narrowed. *Neither did I.* No wonder Margot couldn't wait to get him and Karinne out of the cabin.

"Why didn't you say anything then?" he asked.

"I was nervous. I didn't want to scare Karinne off. My... roommate was eating dinner just outside at the picnic tables."

"I walked right past him?" Karinne swallowed hard as Margot nodded.

"Of course your mother wouldn't be alone all these years," Anita said quickly. "It makes sense that she'd find... friends."

"What's his name?" Cory asked.

Trust Cory to ask the most difficult questions, Max thought to himself. But Cory's questions saved him from asking himself.

"His name is Jonathan—he goes by Jon. Would you like to meet him?"

Karinne flicked a glance at Max. "Of course."

"He's already here. I won't leave him alone." Margot stood and walked over to the closest person at the next table. She laid her hand on the shoulder of a young boy. "My son." A nine-year-old boy looked up—his dark eyes, hair and skin the exact opposite of Margot.

"This is Karinne. Come and give your sister a hug," Margot said.

Karinne faced the young boy, who obediently came over and gave her a shy hug. After a startled moment, Karinne hugged him back. Max brought over the boy's empty chair. The gesture was wasted. Margot gathered the child into her arms, just as she used to do when Karinne was small, to make introductions.

"Hi. Mom told me about you," Jon said to Karinne in comfortable English but with a slight Spanish accent.

"She just told me about you. This is a surprise. I didn't know I had a brother."

Margot avoided Karinne's reproachful gaze.

Jon noticed Karinne's pink sweatshirt. "Mom bought me a brown one like yours," he said. "But I spilled soda on it."

"Don't worry." Margot kissed Jon's cheek. "It'll wash out."

"Cory, why don't you and I go back to the cabin and load up our backpacks?" Anita suggested.

Cory got the hint. He took his tray and Anita's. "I'll check us all out, Max. We'll wait for you at the docks."

"Nice to meet you, Jon," Anita said politely. "See you later."

"Bye," Cory said.

Jon slid out of his mother's lap and sat in an empty chair.

"Did you finish your breakfast?" Margot asked, looking at his plate on the other table.

The boy nodded. "Are we going rafting?"

"If you wish," Max said kindly. The boy's face seemed pale, his manner nervous. "Can you swim?"

"Dad taught me," Jon said.

"Then let's get your gear," Max said, his voice genuinely warm.

Jon actually smiled. "Can we, Mom?"

Max rose and held out Karinne's chair so she could get up. Jon copied Max and did the same for his mother. Max took Karinne's hand. He wished Margot hadn't put him on the spot for an additional two partners rafting, but what other choice did he have? At least the private investigator hadn't found any recent criminal activity on Margot's part. But then, he hadn't learned about this child, either. And he hadn't provided any information about Jon's dad, who was presumably still in the picture.

At their cabin door, Jon said, "I'll do the key, Mom!"

Margot handed him the key, and Jon unlocked the door, leaving it open. "This is Mom's," he said, pointing to the blue backpack. "Mine's brown."

A knock sounded at the open door. Margot looked up, startled, at the two men outside her door. They both wore park ranger green, but they were armed.

"Margot Cavanaugh? Alias Margaret Lazar?"

"I'm Margot."

One of the police officers approached her with a folded paper, while the other readied his handcuffs. "We have a warrant for your arrest."

Phantom Ranch docks

"WHERE ARE THEY?" Cory asked for the third time in ten minutes. He checked his watch, standing on the dock near their raft. "It's been half an hour."

"Maybe Margot needed extra gear, after all," Anita said.

"Even if she did, it wouldn't take Max long to get things organized." Cory snorted. "This whole situation is too bizarre. I'll give him another few minutes. The crowds can't still be holding them up—especially with everyone in the food lines."

"Try your cell phone," Anita suggested. "Or your walkie-talkie."

"What cell? They don't work here, and both radios are stowed in the raft."

Anita took a seat on the dock bench and drew her knees up to her chin. "I don't mind waiting. It'll give Karinne a chance to catch her breath."

"And Max. What a breakfast, huh?" Cory said, sitting beside her. "The woman disappears for years, then comes back to show off her son to Karinne. Talk about a slap in the face."

"It can't be easy for Karinne *or* Jon," Anita observed. "I couldn't tell if he felt like a brother."

"Half brother. I wonder who Jon's father is."

"And where."

"I hope he's not hiding behind the bushes. Next, we'll have *him* begging for a raft ride, too," Cory said with undisguised sarcasm. "I can't take any more shocks on just one cup of coffee. Missing relatives coming out of the closet, new relatives in tow…"

Anita nodded.

Cory leaned over and picked up Anita's hand. "I'm not sure having Margot stay at the apartment is the wisest course of action."

"I'll be up here with you, so I thought it was a nice gesture of Karinne's. You don't want Margot staying with her? Or Jon?"

"No."

"But the three of them could catch up more easily than if Margot's in a hotel. They'd have more privacy."

"Who knows whether Jon comes back for the wedding or not. And don't forget about Jeff."

Anita groaned. "He won't approve at all."

Cory checked his watch again. "Something's wrong. They should've been here by now. I'm going to look for them."

"Not without me," Anita said.

"YOU'RE *ARRESTING* ME?" Margot's voice rose as she backed away from the uniformed couple, male and female park rangers, both armed.

"Yes, ma'am. We'll need to search you."

"Mom?" Karinne said, confused.

"Leave her alone! She didn't do anything!" Jon protested.

The rangers assumed defensive positions. One passed the paperwork to Max and addressed him specifically. "Would you please take these two and wait outside?"

"Of course." Max took Karinne's and Jon's arms and gently propelled them out the still-open front door.

"What are they doing to Mom?" Karinne asked.

"Let me go!" Jon demanded.

"We can't interfere. Let's just find out what's going on first. Then we'll be able to help."

From outside on the porch, Karinne watched in horror as her mother was patted down for weapons, then cuffed, hands behind her back like a common criminal. Jon seemed close to tears, while Margot's face was blank, so expressionless it seemed almost unrecognizable.

One of the rangers handed her a card—her Miranda rights. Max took the copy of the arrest warrant.

"Where are you taking her?" Karinne asked as the trio stepped outside.

"Topside?" Max asked, folding the paper and shoving it in his shirt pocket.

"No, she'll be placed in a holding cell down here. She'll be arraigned and bail set. If it's posted, she could be out as early as tomorrow morning. If not, Mrs. Lazar will be choppered out to the Arizona State P.D. station in the village."

"Grand Canyon Village," the woman elaborated to Jon.

"Mom!" Jon hurried closer, but the two rangers barricaded his way.

"Say goodbye, but please don't touch the prisoner," the man warned.

Karinne immediately took Jon's hand.

"It's okay, Jon," Margot said, finally recovering her voice, her gaze not on Jon but Max. "You called them, didn't you?"

"No," Max said honestly. "But I *will* call a lawyer."

The officers walked Margot away while the crowd stared openly.

"Jon, it's okay. You stay with your sister," Margot ordered. "Karinne, look after him." Karinne's last glimpse of Margot was her turned head as she mouthed, *I love you.*

Jon silently started to cry. Karinne hugged him to her side as the trio drove off.

"She's gone..." Jon whispered.

"She just came back, too..." Karinne managed to say.

"We'll get her out," Max said. He placed a comforting hand on Jon's shoulder and an arm around Karinne's waist. "Let's go inside. Everyone's watching."

Karinne suddenly realized the truth of his words. The door to her mother's cabin remained open, and other hikers and campers continued to stare. She hurried in with Jon, followed by Max, who firmly closed the door against prying eyes. Jon threw himself on the bed, facedown. Karinne gently patted his back, her own eyes teary as Max called his lawyer. Jon calmed down. He eventually sat up, his eyes red.

"Why don't you go in the bathroom and wash your face?" Max said. "Then we'll pack up your clothes, okay?"

Jon nodded and closed the bathroom door.

"We've got to contact the boy's father," Karinne said, wiping her own face.

"Here." Max grabbed some tissues off the nightstand and pressed them into her hand.

"Thanks."

"Since your mother lives in Mexico," Max said, "I'm

assuming her address will be on the paperwork. We'll start there."

Karinne retrieved and unfolded the arrest warrant. "You're right."

Max picked up Margot's backpack and handed it to her. "Perhaps you should get your mother's things together?"

Karinne dropped the paperwork in her lap. "I wonder how the police found her so easily." She looked suspiciously at Max.

"I thought you trusted me, Karinne."

"I thought we were getting married," she countered.

Max exhaled on a heavy sigh. "Those were rangers, Karinne. I didn't call them or the police."

"Then your private detective did!"

"No. Margot's arresting officers were rangers—state agents, not federal. Mexico would have an international warrant, not a local one."

"Then who called the authorities?"

Max's expression was grim. "I wonder if..." He paused. "What about your father?"

"Dad wouldn't..." Karinne's confusion grew. "Would he?"

"Read *why* your mother was arrested, Karinne."

Karinne scanned the paperwork. Her mouth parted in shock, her fingers shaking.

"Bigamy?"

Chapter Eleven

Karinne had finished packing up Margot's clothes by the time Cory and Anita arrived. She and Jon sat outside on the wooden porch steps in front of the cabin, while Max arranged for bail over the phone. Karinne had given Max her credit card, but felt unwilling to leave Jon or make the call herself. Cory and Anita waited inside the cabin with Max.

"When can I see Mom?" the boy asked Karinne.

"Probably tomorrow."

"We have to pay to get her out?"

"Sort of." Karinne didn't think the boy needed the details of posting bond.

"Do you have enough money? 'Cause I've got some, too."

At Jon's innocence, Karinne almost lost her resolve to stay calm. "We have enough, sweetheart. It won't cost much."

The lawyer had informed them that Margot would be arraigned in the morning, and bail was usually a thousand dollars or less. Although illegal in the state of Arizona, bigamy was a class-five felony, as opposed to murder, class one.

"Why is she in jail?" Jon asked. "What's bigamy?"

Karinne thought carefully. "Mom has a...paperwork

problem. The court records say your father and my father are both her husbands."

"But Mom married *my* dad," Jon said.

"I believe you," Karinne assured him.

"What if... What if the police don't?"

"That's why we have to straighten out the paperwork. Once that's done, everything will be fine," she said, not knowing if that was the truth or not. "I'll take care of it—the money part."

"Why?"

"I'm your sister."

"But you don't know me. Mom never told you about me."

"I wish she had."

"I knew about you. She's always talking about *you*."

"We'll talk more. And maybe I'll see you at my wedding."

"I'd like to come, maybe Dad could, too, if you invite him."

"Dad?"

"Stephan Lazar. He works on oil rigs," Jon said proudly. "Mostly Central America. In the summer, when school's out, Mom and I go where he goes."

"The casino lets her take summers off?" Karinne asked curiously.

"Sure. Mom's a good worker. They always want her back. She's been there almost twenty years."

Since she left me and Dad, Karinne realized with a pang.

"Do you have his number?"

"His cell keeps changing, but I know his company's phone number."

"Do you have any other relatives we could call? Uncles, aunts, friends?"

"They're all in Mexico. I don't have their numbers. Mom does."

Karinne saw that Max had hung up. "I'll be right back," she said. She hurried inside the cabin. "What's up?"

"We'll arrange bail tomorrow. We can't get her out until then. I'll call first thing in the morning. Margot won't be transported to a topside facility."

"Thanks, Max. Jon said his father's out of the country. He has a work number for him, but no cell. If service there is as iffy as it is here, I don't know if we can reach him. I'd try, but I understand more Spanish than I speak. You?"

"Not enough for legal matters."

"Maybe your detective could help?"

"I've already contacted him," Max assured her. "Just as I predicted." He shook his head. "Your family takes priority again."

"We'll go down the Colorado again, just you and me," Karinne vowed. "As soon as this is over. With Mom, I mean," she added quickly.

Max didn't reply.

"I'd say the rafting trip is over," Karinne said. "Can we walk Mom and Jon up to the rim tomorrow?"

"The day after. We're not prepared for an eighteen-mile hike. It's uphill, and we haven't packed enough bottled water. We've been filtering and treating river water at camp."

Anita joined them. "Cory told me there are no spare mules. He didn't think there would be, but he checked, anyway."

"Where is Cory?" Max asked.

"Back at the canteen phones. He was hoping to rent a chopper," Anita said. "But no luck there, either. The terminal said it looks pretty nasty. Their forecast says heavy rains tonight and tomorrow."

"If it storms, we're not hiking, either," Max said in a low voice. "I need to talk to Cory about the food supplies. Karinne?"

"Go ahead. I'm going to call my father."

"I'll stay outside with Jon," Anita volunteered.

Karinne crossed the cabin and closed the door for privacy. Her father's phone rang once, twice, then was picked up before the third ring.

"Dad?"

"Hello, Karinne."

"I have some news I need to share."

"If it's about your mother, don't bother. I already heard about it." The tone of his voice told Karinne all she needed to know.

"Dad, you didn't call the police, did you?"

"I most certainly did."

"Why?"

Jeff didn't pretend to misunderstand. "You, of all people, should know the answer to that. Your mother didn't divorce me. Instead, she pretended to die, and put us both through hell. Did the police find her?"

"They had the rangers arrest her. She's in a holding facility here at the bottom of the canyon."

"Good. I hope she spends a year there for every sleepless night we've had."

Karinne flinched at the bitterness in his voice. "Dad… how can you be so cruel?"

"Your mother taught me. At least I've found her, and she'll be in one place long enough for me to divorce her before she disappears again."

Karinne took in a deep breath, the fingers clasping the phone curled tightly. "It's not just about you or me anymore. Margot has a son."

Jeff snorted into the phone. "I don't believe it."

"His name is Jon. He swears Mom and his father are married."

"We both know that's a lie. She's married to me."

"That doesn't mean Mom isn't his mother. Jon has a father somewhere, but he's away and Jon's scared to death."

"Let the police sort it out. He's not my family."

"All the more reason he should be with his mother—and you're forgetting *I'm* his family."

"If she's just the boy's stepmother, you're not."

"She says she's his natural mother, Dad."

"You have no proof. How could you know that for sure?"

"Jon needs me. Mom asked me to take care of him. I said I would."

"My God! She's in jail, and you're stuck with her bastard?"

"She's in jail because of you!"

"She's in jail because of her own actions. Either way, she should've thought of that before. Put him on a plane and send him home, Karinne. Don't let Margot's problems become ours."

"I can't put a child on a plane all by himself! I don't even know where to send him. His father works on oil drills in Central America. We can't reach him. I don't have any idea who the rest of Jon's family is. There's no one to meet him at the airport—no one to take care of him."

"Then turn the boy over to the courts. They'll arrange for care."

"Dad!"

"You might as well know I've contacted the insurance company, too. They're swearing out a civil suit against Margot."

Karinne was horrified. "Mom could end up staying in jail."

"Better her than me. I was the one who cashed your mother's life insurance check, remember? I used it to pay off the mortgage and for your college. I'm not going to jail for insurance fraud."

"But if Mom does, her son will suffer."

"If he's even her son. Either way, I have a clean conscience."

"This will only make things worse," Karinne argued. "I know Mom hurt you—hurt us both—but think of Jon. He's just a kid. At least delay the civil suit until we can track down his father or until Mom's out of the country again."

"Why?" Jeff asked angrily. "So I can risk being held liable for my wife's fraud?"

"No! So her son doesn't go through what I did! Growing up without a mother is hard. Dad, we have to forgive her."

Jeff paused. When he spoke again, he sounded more like the father she'd always known and loved. "Have you, Karinne?"

"I'm trying. Revenge won't bring back the past. We're adults. Jon isn't."

"As adults, we're bound by the law. I have to protect myself, Karinne. Be like me. Draw the line."

Karinne drew in a breath. "I intend to post Mom's bail."

"Then you're as bad as she is. She belongs in prison. Leave her where she is. If she does her disappearing act again before this insurance mess is straightened out, I'm holding you personally responsible."

"Dad, I can't just—"

It was too late. Jeff abruptly hung up, and Karinne replaced the receiver. The irony of the situation was as harsh as Jeff's words.

I've finally found my mother—only to lose my father.

MAX'S HEART ACHED for Karinne as she ended the conversation. She looked almost as pale as the young boy on the cabin steps. Margot's past was wreaking havoc in the present and, he suspected, would continue to do so in the future. For what? Another child's happiness destroyed? Karinne wouldn't walk away from Jon. How could Jeff expect her to? But the only alternative, keeping a guilty woman out of jail, wasn't feasible, either.

"Karinne, are you all right?" Anita asked.

"I've been better."

"Cory, let's go for a walk," Max said to his brother. "Ladies, we won't be long," he told them.

Both men walked away from the cabin, out of earshot of Jon and the women.

"What's up?" Cory asked curiously.

Max quickly explained.

"Margot remarried without a divorce? And Jeff's pressing charges?" Cory exhaled on a slow whistle.

"It gets worse," Max said. "He's already called the insurance company and reported her for fraud. They'll probably be filing civil charges in the next few days."

"How much does she owe?" Cory asked bluntly.

Max told him. Cory whistled again.

"Plus interest and penalties and court fees. Worst-case scenario—Margot goes to jail. Best-case scenario—probation in this country. Either way, she won't be going to Mexico anytime soon."

"What can I do to help?" Cory asked.

"There's no reason you and Anita need to go through this. You could take Anita safely up to the rim. We can spare enough bottled water for that. I'll have to buy more for the rest of us."

Cory crossed his arms. "Then what? Raft Margot down the Colorado and smuggle her into Mexico?"

"Very funny," Max said irritably.

"Well…" Cory paused significantly. "Once she's free tomorrow, what's to stop her from skipping bail and disappearing again?"

"She has to get back to civilization first. Karinne and I can get her and Jon topside later and get them to the lawyer. You and Anita should go on ahead now."

"Anita won't agree once she knows what's going on. She'll want to be there for Karinne. And I can't just leave, either," Cory insisted. "You might need me. I'll stick around."

"Thanks," Max said.

Chapter Twelve

The next day, outside Margot's cabin, Karinne set out fruit, trail mix and boxed drinks for herself, Anita and Jon. She wasn't hungry, but breakfast had been a failure, and preparing snacks was something to do. She'd packed up her mother's clothing except for a single fresh outfit. The men had left under dark gray skies to finish the legal paperwork, post bail and bring Margot back to the cabin.

The weather didn't add any cheer. Even the canyon colors seemed washed out, muddy. Originally, Karinne wanted to hike with Max to the temporary holding cell in the bottom of the canyon, which was mostly used for the drunk and disorderly.

"You and I can go post bail, Max," Karinne suggested.

Jon immediately grabbed Karinne's hand. "Me, too."

"No, son, I think you should stay here," Max said. "You, too, Karinne. Margot won't want Jon—or you—to see her in a jail cell."

"Why don't I go with Max?" Cory volunteered.

Karinne nodded her agreement.

"We'll be back soon," he said.

"How soon?" Jon asked Max.

"I'm not sure. More than an hour, depending on the paperwork, plus the hike. Two hours, tops." He kissed

Karinne's cheek and squeezed Jon's shoulder. "Don't hold lunch for us. You're in charge, big guy."

Jon brightened a little, but he didn't eat any more breakfast than Karinne or Anita. Hence, the snacks. They remained untouched, still wrapped at the picnic table. Karinne absently shooed away the occasional fly and waited.

MAX DIDN'T TAKE his usual brisk steps to the ranger station.

"Why so slow? You okay?" Cory asked. The holding cell was a half-hour walk at a fast clip.

"Yeah. Just wondering if Margot's trustworthy enough not to skip bail. The P.I. told me she had a gambling problem."

"So you said."

"Margot was gambling before she disappeared. I wonder if she still is."

"Thank heaven there's no casinos down here."

"I'd hate for Karinne to lose her bail money," Max said.

"Does Margot know you've hired a detective?"

"Oh, she'll know. I'll make sure of that."

"Good for you," Cory said. "And…"

"I'm waiting for more information. The detective agency has nothing valid from Arizona, no surprise there. He's still checking in Mexico."

"Maybe she's just sleeping with the boyfriend, this Lazar, and keeping up appearances for her son's sake."

"That's a definite possibility," Max said as the men hiked side by side.

"That would be one legal problem solved for Margot. Although I don't suppose she can lie to Jon about her marriage to Jeff forever."

"Even without bigamy charges, Margot's still liable to

the insurance company. None of this explains why she suddenly reappears to see a daughter she abandoned years ago. Why bring her lover's son? Or risk legal proceedings?" Max asked. "She has everything to lose."

"Maybe she's gambled away all her money again, and she's here to get money out of Karinne. She couldn't post bail. She needs Karinne's credit card for that."

"It's more than money. Margot had enough to get her and Jon all the way here from Mexico and back."

"I don't care. I'm still watching my wallet," Cory warned. "You should, too. You know…I have an idea." Cory grabbed at Max, stopping their progress. "Let's pretend to lose Karinne's credit card—and keep Margot here a bit longer until the detective finds out more."

"Tempting…but no. Besides, I plan to use my own credit card."

"Noble, but stupid, Max."

"Yeah, well, everything I do when it comes to Karinne is stupid."

"What's that supposed to mean?"

"You might as well know the wedding is off."

"*What?* Karinne called it off?"

"No, I did."

Cory waited until some of the closer hikers passed them by and they had privacy.

"What happened?" Cory asked, his forehead lined with concern. "I thought you loved her."

"I do…always have. But it's obvious she doesn't need me, Cory. Doesn't want me. Doesn't want children. I guess I need more than just the words."

"What did Karinne say?"

"She's still in denial. Then her mother showed up and—"

"God, Max, I'm sorry."

Max shrugged. "Speaking of her mother, let's pick up the pace. We don't have all day."

They reached the jail in good time and started the procedure that would set Margot free. In under an hour, Max, Cory and a weary Margot were outside the holding cell on the trail that would take them back to the others. The two men walked on either side of Margot.

"How's Jon?" Margot immediately asked once they were under way.

"Good," Max said. "He's with Karinne, of course."

"We left him eating breakfast at the cabin," Cory added.

"And Karinne? Is she okay?"

"She is," Max replied.

"I hope Jon's not too worried," Margot fretted.

"Yeah, don't worry about your daughter," Cory said with disgust. "Listen, I'll hurry over to the cabin and tell them both that you're coming."

Cory jogged ahead on the trail, obviously eager to escape Margot. Meanwhile, she shifted nervously from one foot to the other, her face pale.

"Would you like some water?" Max asked.

"No, my back's just stiff. Let's keep walking."

Max offered his arm. After a pause, Margot took it as they negotiated crowds of people on the footpath.

"The prison bunks aren't very comfortable. It's the first time I've ever been in one. I hope it's the last."

Margot shivered and her fingers around his arm seemed cold. They slowed to a necessary stop as the crowd bottlenecked around a scenic curve. Everyone was actively on the move, and Max took advantage of the empty benches.

"Why don't we take a breather."

He led Margot off the trail to a place in the shade beneath some cottonwoods. There, he removed his canteen and offered it as Margot sat.

She took a few swallows and held it in her lap. "I guess I was thirsty after all," she admitted.

"Did you eat anything yesterday?"

"Not much. I was too upset."

Margot had another sip of water, then screwed on the cap and handed the canteen back to Max.

"Who called the police on me? I know it wasn't Karinne. *Was* it you?"

"No. It was Jeff."

"I should've guessed."

"Karinne talked to him earlier and told him you'd resurfaced," Max confirmed. "I'm sorry."

"So am I." Margot paused. "If you have any questions, ask them now," she said abruptly.

"Excuse me?"

"You've been kind to me and my son—almost as kind as Karinne."

"I'm not sure about that."

"The guard said you posted bail, not Karinne. Thank you. I promise I'll pay you back."

"You should know that Karinne wanted to post bail herself," Max said. "She gave me her credit card."

"Then why use yours?"

Max shrugged. "The important thing is that you're out of there. Can I ask you a personal question?"

"Ask me anything. If I can answer, I will."

Max searched for a tactful way to broach the subject. "You mentioned a second husband. I didn't know you divorced Jeff."

"I haven't. The bigamy charge wouldn't stand up in court, despite Jeff's claims. He jumped the gun. I was just protecting Jon. But I could hardly explain that to the rangers in front of my children. If they even would've listened."

"So your second marriage is...?"

"A pretense, of course."

"I wondered about that."

"You never trusted easily, Max."

"In my job, caution gets to be a habit. That's why I hired someone to check out your background."

"Why?"

"I felt I had to," Max admitted. "When you first called me, you asked for money. And there were discrepancies in your story. The investigator didn't say you still worked as a photographer."

"I didn't say I took photos for pay. I photograph Jon."

"Semantics, Mrs. C. Semantics. You work in a casino— not a good job for someone with a gambling problem."

"You did get your money's worth, Max. And I'm not gambling anymore."

Max frowned. "How did you pass the background check for the casino?"

"I used my real name. We're not talking Las Vegas or Monte Carlo," Margot said dryly. "I'm very good at spotting cardsharps. I used to be one."

"And Stephan Lazar?"

"We met in the casino. When I started, I worked the floor, making sure players at the blackjack and poker tables weren't cheating. I graduated to the cameras upstairs. But before that, I met Jon's father. The oil workers came in every payday. They were a pretty honest group. Stephan noticed me and we began dating. One thing led to another..."

"To Jon?"

"Yes. I wasn't planning on it, but I wanted the baby. I also knew Jeff wouldn't want me back. At first I didn't tell Stephan I was pregnant. Finally I had to say something or break off my relationship with him—I couldn't hide it forever. So I pretended to be widowed, but said I couldn't remarry without losing my widow's pension. Stephan argued that I wouldn't need it, that he'd provide for me, but I convinced him I couldn't give up my imaginary pension. He accepted that, eagerly laid claim to his son and calls me his wife. Stephan's a good man. I agreed to move in with him two months before Jon was due."

"Does Stephan know about Karinne?"

"Yes. So does Jon. I told them my grown daughter travels frequently."

"You told *them,* but not Karinne...." Max shook his head, feeling bad for the unknown "husband" but worse for Karinne.

"So I'm a coward. But I believed concealing the truth was best for my new family."

"Why the cloak-and-dagger routine? Why break your silence after all these years?"

"I didn't want to miss Karinne's wedding."

Max looked directly at her. "It isn't for months yet."

She sighed. "I know."

"Then why bring Jon? You told me to ask, Margot. So I'm asking. Why are you *really* here?"

"To save my son. He's sick."

"Sick? Jon didn't seem ill to me."

Margot hesitated. "Earlier this year, Jon was hospitalized for a prolonged, severe case of the flu. It was viral, but he just couldn't seem to shake it. The lab work came back with red flags."

"Go on."

"The doctors discovered he was born with a problem kidney. The tests show signs of CKD—chronic kidney disease. It's a progressive loss of renal functions. It can take anywhere from months to years to develop, but eventually causes renal failure. In Jon's case, we're talking months."

"I'm sorry. Does Jon know?"

"Of course he does, but he doesn't realize how sick he could get."

"Then why risk your son's health—"

"I would never do that!" Margot said angrily. "The doctors said he could fly."

"To reunite Jon with a sister he's never seen?"

"Jon's going to need a new kidney soon."

"You said he had a problem kidney. Singular. What's wrong with the other?"

"He was born with only one."

Max suddenly understood where the conversation was going. He recapped the canteen.

"The doctors said Jon needs a kidney transplant. It doesn't matter if it comes from an adult or child. I'd give him one of mine, but I'm not a match. Down the road, when things get worse, he can hold on with medication and dialysis, but not forever."

"So you *didn't* come for our wedding. You came back for, what, spare parts?" Max felt his stomach drop at the ghoulishness of the situation.

Margot flushed. "If Karinne and Jon are a tissue match, Jon has a fighting chance. It would be perfectly safe for her."

"No surgery is *perfectly safe*."

"She can live a normal life with one kidney."

"She could die." He went cold at the very thought.

"*Jon* could die! Do you think I'd risk so much and come so far if there were any other choice?"

"Karinne didn't say anything about this to me."

"I haven't told her yet."

Which was what he'd suspected. Margot's presence

seemed to be pulling him and Karinne further apart. She hadn't mentioned her mother and the sweatshirt; he hadn't told Karinne about the phone calls and hiring a detective. And now this...

"I've answered all your questions," Margot said. "I'd like you to answer one for me."

Max raised his head.

"When I came to your house years ago and asked where Karinne was, you said you didn't know."

"That's what I said."

"I've wondered all these years—was it the truth?"

"No. I lied."

Margot blanched. "Where was she?"

"Inside the house, playing with Cory."

"So close." Margot looked near tears. "You have no idea of the grief you caused me. I would've taken her with me, you know."

He didn't respond.

"Why did you lie, Max? You were always honest."

"Because, Mrs. C, somehow I knew...you weren't."

Chapter Thirteen

Karinne saw her mother and Max from a distance and ran to greet them. She hugged her mother first, and then Max.

"Thank you," she whispered. "How is she?"

"A little rough around the edges, but she'll be fine."

Karinne gave Max a final squeeze, and then turned back toward Margot. Her release from jail, and the subsequent mother-son reunion, brought smiles to everyone's faces. Max felt better seeing the boy perk up. Having one's mother in jail had to be traumatic. He hoped that the stress of this trip wouldn't have any physical impact on the boy, either. He wondered how Karinne was doing. Margot had left her daughter as a young child, then returned only because of her second child; Karinne would soon find that out.

He noticed that she hadn't smiled lately. He could hardly blame her. So far, Margot's appearance had them turning to private investigators and to others, not each other.

And thanks to Margot, Karinne would be distracted as they rafted downriver, during her first real opportunity to learn about his job. While he hardly expected to compete with a reappearing mother and unknown brother, or Jeff with his heart condition, it seemed that there was always *something* impinging on whatever time he did get with Karinne.

It was just as well that he'd stopped dreaming, stopped hoping for a future for them as husband and wife. That thought hurt, and he suspected it would continue to do so. But all in all, it was for the best. He wanted a woman who was committed to him heart and soul. He refused to be an afterthought or an also-ran. Perhaps it was his own fault. He'd been the older friend, almost a big brother to Karinne as well as Cory growing up. And despite their physical relationship as mature adults, Karinne seemed to take him for granted. He was in the background of her life, the guy she could always count on.

He shook off those gloomy thoughts and replenished the woodpile while Margot showered and changed into fresh clothes. Inside, Karinne kept her mother company. Max and Cory remained out on the porch. Anita and Jon poked around back, searching for and identifying animal life. Max took the opportunity to quietly update Cory on what he'd learned from Margot and his private detective.

"Let me get this straight," Cory said, stacking his load. "Margot played dead, never got divorced, but says she's pretending marriage to the new guy. So the second husband's not a husband...just Jon's father?"

"Who thinks he's living with a widow. When Karinne repeated Margot's story about the marriage to her own father, Jeff obviously jumped to conclusions," Max said. "Hence the bigamy charge."

"At least she won't need a lawyer or a court appearance to deal with that." Cory shrugged. "So Margot saw your wedding announcement and invited herself—and her son. How's she been keeping tabs on Karinne...newspaper by-lines? The internet?"

"Both, I suspect. But Margot isn't here for the wedding. That's months away—not that it'll even happen. Margot's on a treasure hunt. And Karinne's the treasure."

"Now you've lost me."

Max explained, concluding with, "Jon needs a kidney transplant. Margot's not a match. She's hoping Karinne is."

"What about his father's side of the family? Has she asked them? Let Margot play vulture around *those* people, not Karinne," Cory said indignantly. "How did Margot even know Karinne was here at the canyon?"

"The detective says Margot and Jon were our tour's last-minute cancellation," Max said. "And we did just what she'd hoped we do—asked Karinne and Anita to take the vacant space."

"That detective should be getting more family medical records. Karinne goes under the knife, or Karinne goes to her brother's funeral. Some choice. Who could say no?"

"I don't know if Karinne can—unless it's a ruse to get money, and I don't think it is," Max said. "Margot sounded pretty desperate, but she hasn't told Karinne yet."

"You should call the police again. If she's telling the truth, it's close to extortion."

"Karinne wouldn't press charges against her mother. Margot comes first," Max said, his brows meeting in disapproval.

Cory broke some long, dry kindling over his thigh. "I'll bet Jeff would press charges. He's already proved that much. Did you tell him about Jon's kidney problem?"

"No, I just found out. Besides, the man's got heart problems. That's the last thing he needs to know right now. But I suppose someone will have to tell him if Karinne's a tissue match."

"Half siblings...I dunno, Max," Cory said. "Is it even possible? I mean, they might as well be strangers."

"That's irrelevant as far as donor compatibility goes. Besides, Karinne and Margot aren't strangers," Max said grimly. "Gods knows what those two are talking about in there."

Max gestured toward the closed cabin door. Anita and Jon were laughing in the distance, playing pirates with two brown sticks as swords.

"If Jon's sick, how did he and Margot get down to us from topside?" Cory asked.

"The mules. Margot's rented the cabin for two more days."

"I saw she had two mules reserved for the trip up when I was checking for cancellations," Cory confirmed.

"Which means she's been planning this for some time."

Cory lowered his voice even more. "With a sick child, I'm sure Margot's not staying around until the wedding. It's in the fall."

"There's not going to be any wedding, remember?"

Cory sighed. "You've got to tell Karinne about this whole donor idea—before Margot puts her own particular spin on it."

"I'm sure I won't have to," Max said. "Margot's telling Karinne as we speak. She doesn't waste an opportunity, that woman."

"You're probably right." Cory thumped his brother on the shoulder in sympathy. "I guess the raft trip is over."

"That's what I've been trying to say. You and Anita don't have to hang around. Hike on up to the rim."

"Not without you and Karinne. Max...are you really calling it off? Isn't there any chance you two will patch things up?"

"About as much chance as Margot and Jeff living happily ever after," Max said grimly.

KARINNE SAT on Jon's bed—her brother's bed—in shock at the news. She could hardly fathom Margot's story.

"So…you found a new family? You remarried?"

"No, because I never got divorced. Stephan doesn't know that." Margot sat next to her in bare feet. Barefoot but otherwise dressed, Margot pulled on clean socks. That everyday, ordinary task seemed out of place with such momentous news, at least to Karinne. Margot had apparently spent the first decade of her new life gambling, working—in casinos, no less—and gambling some more.

"Oh, Mom." Her mother's whole life had been a lie, first with her original family, then with her new one.

Margot's carefree existence had suddenly changed when she met Jon's father.

"Stephan was the first man since Jeff I was really serious about. I didn't rush things, but I missed having someone. Eventually Stephan and I had sex—safe sex, of course. Who doesn't these days? I didn't plan to get pregnant. Jon was a definite surprise, but it didn't matter. Stephan was my chance for a fresh start."

"Without Dad or me?"

"Stephan wanted to be part of raising the baby, and I was lonely. After ten years of the night life, I was drained. I wanted a regular life, a family. I missed the early days when I was happily married…but not the years when your father and I were fighting." She sat down again next to Karinne, the shoes in her lap. "I had—have—a gambling problem, as I told you. Back then, it wasn't under control. Jeff threatened to divorce me and take full custody of you."

Karinne stared.

"I think I went crazy," Margot said. "I started gambling even more, and that's when I lost the house. I didn't know what to do."

"You could have asked for *help!*"

"I was past help. I love you, Karinne. I wanted my daughter to remember the woman I was, instead of the wife and mother who threw it all away at the blackjack tables."

"Max said you wanted money from him. Why, Mom?"

"Not for gambling! Only for false ID to get into this country under an assumed name. I couldn't afford it, and I didn't dare ask Stephan for the money. To him, I'm a widow, Mrs. *Jeff Cavanaugh*. But I go by Margaret Lazar now."

"How did you get into the U.S.?" Karinne demanded. "If you didn't have ID?"

"I told the border officials I was a Mexican citizen. I had Jon's birth certificate to back me up. And it's what Stephan believes me to be."

"In other words, you've committed fraud again. That's an awfully big risk for someone who quit gambling. Or have you?"

"I am gambling, Karinne, but not on cards or dice—on *you*. I told you Jon was my son. I didn't tell you he has a serious kidney problem. He could die. You could be a donor match for him. I'm not."

"Just on your say-so, I'm to believe this?"

"He's your biological *half brother*," Margot emphasized. "Any DNA test will prove it. You can do the compatibility test at the same time. I have a copy of Jon's medical records. I'll let you see them."

"Compatibility?" Karinne swallowed hard. "What about Stephan? What about his family? Don't they want to help?"

"Of course they do! But they aren't matches, either. We've tested everyone, Karinne, except you."

Karinne didn't know what to think. "Why isn't Stephan here with you?" she asked suspiciously.

"He can't leave his job and risk losing medical coverage. Will you get the blood test?"

"Fine. I'll get the labs done—for Jon, not for you."

"And if they match, will you be a donor?" Margot begged, reaching for daughter's hand.

"I'll consider it—if he's truly my brother."

"He is." Margot's shoes fell on the floor as she hugged Karinne tightly. "I knew you wouldn't let me down. Thank you, darling."

Karinne didn't pull away, nor could she make herself hug her mother back. She studied Margot with new eyes and suddenly understood how her gentle father could get so angry. She felt volatile herself, full of rage and despair, hate and love. She needed fresh air. But as she opened the door, Jon, Anita, Cory and Max rushed inside. Despite the earlier promise of sun, dangerous sheets of monsoon rain suddenly cascaded from above. A huge gust of wind ripped a half-dead tree from the ground and flung it through the foursome's cabin's side, shattering boards and glass. At the sound of it, Max and Cory hurried outside, slickers on. They soon returned with bad news.

"Our cabin's taken a hit, people. We're all stuck here for the night."

THE RAIN CONTINUED to fall in torrents hours after it had begun and well into the night, forcing everyone to stay sheltered due to the violence of the storm. The rain wouldn't let up into lighter individual droplets; it poured sheets of solid water that beat on the cabin's roof and drowned out the popping of logs in the fireplace. The tepid rain became colder with the onset of darkness, and the chilly dampness in the cabin was only partially lessened by the fire's glow.

Karinne watched for Max's return. He'd gone out into the rain to check the level of the Colorado and the water saturation of the camping area. They'd alternated every few hours getting wood. In one bed mother and son were sleeping. Anita lay in the other. Karinne sat at the foot, but neither woman's eyes were closed. Cory slouched in front of the fire, his elbow resting on the raised rock hearth.

Karinne was awake; she felt glad Jon and Margot were asleep, but wished Max would hurry back. She didn't like to think of him out in the elements. While she knew they didn't frighten him, she also knew that nature often claimed the upper hand.

"You're soaked," Cory said when Max eventually returned. "Take my place by the fire."

"The river's still rising?" Karinne handed him a towel and dry shirt as Max took Cory's spot.

"Yes, but that's to be expected."

Anita sat up in bed. "We're safe here, right?"

"We're okay for now. Still...the water's up to my ankles in places, and down by the docks it's deeper. Nor is the rain letting up. This isn't a regular rain shower, people. This is an early monsoon."

"Did you swing by the ranger cabin, Max?" Cory asked.

"Yes. They hadn't bedded down for the night. If the rain doesn't decrease by morning, the evac flag goes up, they said."

"What about—" Karinne gestured toward the bed where her mother and brother slept. "They have mule rides reserved."

Max rubbed the towel over his dripping head and face. "The mules won't be coming down tomorrow. The rangers said the mule train will stay topside, along with any riders."

Cory frowned. "We can't hike in a monsoon. Safety would be a problem."

"A big problem," Max agreed. "The weather would make the main trail impassable. Come first light, I'll bring our raft inland—in case we have to navigate to higher ground."

Karinne's spirits sank. "Higher ground? Is it that bad? The river's dammed."

"Yes, but we still have to deal with actual rainfall between dams."

"These cabins were built up off the ground," Anita observed.

"Just a few feet. I'd rather not take chances," Max said.

"But you said the water was only ankle-deep," Cory said.

"If the rain doesn't let up, I'll be surprised to find the dock above water in the morning. I'd hate to lose the raft," Max said. "We definitely might need it."

"Or the life jackets," Anita added nervously.

"No one should go to the dock now," Karinne argued. "It's too dark."

"I don't plan on it, unless the water level outside gets too high," Max said.

"What about calling for the weather forecast? Is the phone still working?" Anita asked.

Cory, closest to the receiver, lifted it up and set it down again. "It's working, but why bother? Listen to the wind! It's blowing the rain sideways."

"We're getting close to gale-force winds," Max confirmed. "I saw more trees down last time I was out."

Jon mumbled in his sleep and turned restlessly. No one spoke again until Jon quieted.

"As long as the trees don't come through this roof, we have food and a dry place to sleep," Cory said.

"Not much dry wood left, though." They'd taken turns going out to the shoulder-high stack, and Karinne had gone last. The overhang on the roof wasn't an effective shelter from the wind. "I had to dig deep into the middle of the stack."

"We'll keep the coals going and burn it wet," Max said.

"Can we do that?" Anita asked uneasily.

"Sure, if we stoke it carefully. Even without a fire, we won't freeze," Cory assured her, then stifled a yawn.

"I'll take the first shift," Max said.

"I'll keep you company," Karinne volunteered. She and Cory traded places, Cory resting next to his wife on the bed, Karinne beside Max by the hearth.

The wind continued to howl. At times rain pelted the windows like pebbles. Karinne's ears were aching; the storm echoed with a deeper, hollow bass amplified in the canyon and the one-room cabin. That moaning sound, rather than the contrasting high shrieks of wind or drumming rain, drew out goose bumps on Karinne's arms.

"Now I know why the Anasazi preferred cliff dwellings," Anita said, her hands over her ears.

"Use the cotton balls in the first aid kit," Cory suggested.

Cory retrieved some for Anita, and seconds later her ears were stuffed. Cory used some himself, tossed Max the first aid kit, then settled Anita's head on his shoulder.

Max held the kit out to her. "You need some, Karinne?"

Karinne shook her head. "I want to hear the storm."

"So do I."

The howling increased as the wind shifted slightly down the canyon. "I don't understand how Jon can sleep through it. Margot, either."

"The boy seems quite calm under the circumstances. How are you?"

"I think we should call the ranger station for another update," Karinne said.

"Cory listened to the recording a few minutes ago." Max sat close, but made no move to swing his arm around her waist as he usually would've done. "There's no new update. The rangers left the station for an emergency. Too bad they couldn't stay sheltered and wait it out."

Karinne thought of the narrow trail leading to the rim. There were places where even two hikers couldn't walk abreast.

"I wonder when Mom booked a flight back to Mexico," Karinne murmured. "Or even if she did."

"I doubt it. I can't see Margot leaving until she gets what she wants. She has a sick son, and she's decided you're his salvation. Do you think she was telling the truth?"

"About that, yes." Karinne flushed, embarrassed for her mother. "And I thought she really wanted to see me. I even bought her line about wanting to be at our wedding. Which you say isn't going to happen."

"I wonder if she ever intended to show up, regardless of your invitation."

"You don't approve of it?"

"First Jeff was your priority. Then Margot. Now Jon. I don't think I've ever been important in your life, Karinne, or you wouldn't keep pushing me aside. In fact, you've never even asked for my advice or opinion during this whole mess. Margot shows up, and I'm shoved into the background. Again. How do you think that makes me feel?"

Karinne gripped the edges of the hearth, the roughness of the rock imprinting itself into her palms. "I said I'd give up my job if you'd give up the idea of having children."

"You said you'd think about it."

"I agreed to get Dad professional care."

"That was your desperate attempt to salvage our

relationship. Just like this trek down the Colorado with you was mine. I'm just the friend next door you've taken for granted ever since your mother disappeared. A security blanket."

"You never said any of this before, Max."

"Yes, I did. You just never listened. So I waited. And like I told you, I'm tired of waiting."

"What would you have me do? Give up my professional dreams? Ignore my family?"

He shook his head. "I never wanted anything from you under duress. I hoped you'd choose to be with me because you wanted to, just like I wanted to be with you."

"I *do* want to be with you," Karinne said fiercely.

Max's smile was bitter. "Even though you'd delay the wedding a third time, so Margot can slice you to pieces? *Literally.*"

Chapter Fourteen

The wind and the rain still fell into the canyon. Those awake in the cabin weren't surprised when the lights went out. It wasn't until the predawn hours that the wind's heavy gusts lessened, replaced by the steady sound of rain falling. The sputtering fire shone on Max, asleep on the floor. Karinne sat beside him, the flashlight at her side. Cory had brought in the last load of wood, and Karinne was due to bring in the next. She couldn't have slept, anyway, reviewing the conversation she'd had with Max.

"So I should just let the boy die?" Karinne had asked.

"I'm saying don't jump into anything until you've investigated all your options. Most organ donors go through weeks—months—of counseling before reputable hospitals agree to transplants. Margot's been missing for years. We don't even know where she intends to have this transplant done. Here? Mexico? Another galaxy? Who's going to look out for *your* interests? Margot's already shown that it's not *her* first priority."

You'll let her slice you to pieces...literally.

His words had been said in anger, but they had the ring of truth. Max had thrown her seriously off-kilter. Karinne hadn't been so on edge since her "late" mother's memorial service, not even at Margot's miraculous return. Margot's appearance had chased away the adult Karinne and resurrected that sad little girl from the past. She felt a child's emotions, a child's confusion. Her whole world churned as violently as the Colorado white waters when she remembered Max's words.

Margot's emotionally blackmailing you.

Of course she was. Karinne could admit it and even understand it. She *didn't* understand why Margot could fight so hard for Jon now, and not Karinne years ago. Margot could have faced her husband, Jeff, and confessed her gambling problem. Nor was Max's part in preventing Margot from spiriting away the young Karinne any excuse. Margot should never have planned to leave, never planned to take Karinne away from her father and her home. Max was right; she shouldn't trust Margot any more than he did.

Margot had two children. Could she really sacrifice one for the other? Her mother's tumultuous reappearance would never change Karinne's feelings for the man she loved—but Jon's condition could change everyone's future....

Max had made some valid points, however. If no one in Stephan's family was a match, why couldn't Jon get a transplant from the anonymous donor list? Surely Mexico's medical protocol took young children into account. Kidney transplants weren't as rare or dangerous as other kinds of transplants. Jon certainly didn't look sick, but if Margot was being honest, how could Karinne condemn a child to death—one who was her own brother?

I feel like running away myself, Karinne thought. The irony of the situation didn't escape her. *I'm my mother's daughter, after all.*

An uncharacteristic wave of hopelessness swept over her. Everyone wanted someone else to make concessions, so they could live happily ever after. Jeff needed Karinne to stay in Phoenix; Max needed to stay in the canyon and wanted her there; Margot needed Karinne to sacrifice a kidney for her son.

Karinne checked the fire. It was her turn to watch the coals. She'd need more wood, but as she got up, Max rose from his stretched-out position on the floor, and caught her hand.

"We've got enough for now," he said quietly.

"I assumed you were asleep."

"Just resting my eyes. I wasn't sleeping."

Karinne looked out the window. "I wish the sun would come up. I want to go home."

Max frowned. "I thought you wanted to stay with your mother and brother."

"I should take them to see my father."

"I don't think that's a scene Jon needs." Max gently pulled her down, with a familiar kindness she'd grown to rely on. Karinne sat cross-legged on one half of the quilted nylon, Max on the other.

"I should go back to Phoenix and get to a hospital," Karinne said slowly. "If I'm a match for Jon, I want to help."

"That's another scene Jon can skip. I doubt your father's going to approve."

"The way you don't approve?"

"You've always had a big heart, Karinne. It's one of the things I love about you. I think your desire to save a life, especially the life of a child, is commendable. However, I also think that isn't something that can be decided on the spur of the moment."

Karinne shook her head. "Yet you decided the wedding was off on the spur of the moment. We could still have gone through with it. At the worst, we could have delayed it."

"Delayed it? How long? Until this thing with Jon is settled? Until you work out your feelings for your mother? Until we're both old and gray and too old to have children?"

"I meant postpone the wedding for a few months," Karinne said before she lost her nerve. "A few more if Jon and I are a match, and I have surgery. And then I'd have to recover—and get reacquainted with Mom."

Max's voice grew harsh. "Sounds less like months and more like years."

"There's still my dad's health to consider," Karinne said.

"We'll just add a decade or two onto the final total. You don't want to get married at all, Karinne. Why not have the guts to admit it?"

"I'm not staying that! I love you, and I know you love me. But my father needs me. So do Jon and my mother."

"So we wait until everyone's given a clean bill of health?"

"Yes. Is that asking too much?"

"Your father's elderly. He's not going to get younger. Forgive my bluntness, but death is the only cure for old age."

Karinne gasped.

"As for your brother, health and happiness may not be just around the corner, either. What if you're not donor material?"

"Max," she said, "*you're* the one who doesn't want to go through with the wedding. But you're accusing me of that."

"Why would I want a marriage that exists in name only? Where we maintain the status quo in separate towns? That's not what a marriage should be. It hardly fits the definition of family."

"I care about my family!"

"Do they care just as much about you?" Max asked sharply. "Have you asked Margot exactly *when* Jon needs a kidney? He couldn't be here if he needed it immediately and was on the waiting list. You'd delay our wedding again and you don't even know the time frame. Margot hasn't mentioned a word about it to me. You?"

"Well…I just figured…the sooner the better."

"I doubt she's even put him on the list." He sighed. "You want to save Jon? Fine, save him, but don't wait for your sacrifice to make Margot love you. You wanna be a donor? Make sure you're not Margot's easiest way out."

"That can't be true." Karinne felt sick to her stomach. "Mom would've made sure he was on the list, I'm positive."

"How do you know? Did you *ask* her? No. Did Margot volunteer the information? No, again. Why do you think I hired a detective? There may be other, more timely matches for Jon on the donor list. She's risking your health…yes. But she's also risking Jon's by bringing him all the way here from Mexico. Can't you see, Karinne? Once again Margot's putting herself instead of her child first. I never trusted her when I was a boy, and I don't trust her now. Be careful before you play the hero."

"I see. Only you can play that role, like saving me from being used by my evil mother. Or holding my hand when I'm acting stupid."

"The one without your ring?" Max picked up her hand and dropped it. "Don't think I haven't noticed. And I'm not the one being a hero, Karinne. You won't leave your father, which makes it easy for him to stay alone in that big house instead of swallowing his pride, showing how unselfishly he could love his daughter and moving into an assisted care facility. You have all these people to save—except yourself. I can admire your loyalty, Karinne. Except it seems that your loyalty to me, our relationship as a couple, is the price we're paying."

The fire popped and abruptly settled, the main log

breaking and sending sparks flying. Karinne stood awkwardly. Max remained seated.

"We need more wood," she said.

Karinne stepped away and lifted her jacket from on top of her backpack. She shrugged it on and hurried to the door as his voice rang out in one last sentence.

"Running away won't solve anything." Max watched Karinne close the door.

"GO AFTER HER," Cory ordered.

"She's getting firewood," Max said, his voice dull. "She doesn't need me for that."

"What you did was stupid, Max!" Margot spoke from where she lay on the bed.

"I thought you were sleeping," he said.

"I was listening. You can't ask Karinne to choose between her family and you."

"He never has," Cory spat out. "It's bad enough that Jeff refuses to take care of himself. Now you and Jon want a piece of Karinne. She can spend the rest of her life lonely and miserable, just like she spent her childhood. Is that what you want, Margot? Go after her, Max!"

"Just tell her things will be okay, and you'll give her time," Margot suggested.

"You *always* take the easy way, Margot. You're doing it now. I hope you treat your son better!" Cory said.

"Lower your voice. You'll wake him! And I'm doing my best for my son," Margot hissed.

"By using Karinne as a donor?" Max asked.

"I can't help Jon myself," Margot said to Cory. "I'm not a match."

"Is Jon on the waiting list for a kidney? Did you give him a chance to be saved by someone else?" Max asked.

Margot didn't say anything.

"I have my answer," he said.

"Figures." Cory's voice was filled with disgust. "You're a gambler, Mrs. C. You prefer to make your own luck. Why wait for some random donor when you can stack the deck with Karinne? You don't care whose life you wreck."

"I care more than your brother did when I went to talk to my daughter for the last time. He wouldn't even let me see her."

"That was years ago. You didn't have to leave, and Max did what had to be done," Cory said harshly. "I wish you'd never come here."

"Cory!" By now Anita was awake.

"You and Jeff were lousy parents! We knew it then, and we were just *kids*. The two of you are still bad parents."

"Cory, enough!" Max ordered. "All of you...*where's Jon?*"

Everyone looked around.

"Someone check the bathroom."

Cory slammed open the door of the bathroom and emerged, his face worried. "He's not in there, Max."

Max and Cory scrambled for flashlights.

"Anita?" Cory asked. "Did you see him leave?"

Anita shook her head. "I wasn't paying attention."

"Oh, my God, he must've heard us," Margot whispered as Max shone the light under the bunks and into the kitchen. "Where did he go?"

"Where younger brothers always go for help," Cory said, catching his brother's gaze. "Their older sibling."

Anita stared at Cory. "Karinne?"

"Who else? She went out to get wood. Jon must have followed after overhearing our conversation."

As Max silently pulled on his boots, Margot began to cry.

Cabin Fox-5

OUTSIDE, VISIBILITY lightened just enough for Karinne to make it to the woodpile without a flashlight, but not enough to pierce the misting rain and dark shadows down in the canyon walls. The remaining scraps of wood at the bottom of their cabin's pile had sunk into the soft mud, making them totally useless. Max had already brought in the last of the wood at Deer-15, their own cabin. The search for new fireplace fuel would give her an excuse for a temporary escape.

Karinne kept hearing Max's words over and over in her head. Margot had sacrificed Karinne's childhood for selfish reasons. Now Margot wanted to sacrifice her for Jon. She continued to hike, her mind racing as she trudged along the mucky trail among the widely spaced lodgings, past the empty woodpiles of the Bear and Cougar cabins and toward the Deer and Elk areas.

By the time she finally reached Fox-5's cabin and porch, Karinne was shivering. Despite her jacket, she felt cold, her boots muddy and socks soggy. She vaguely knew she had to stop, warm up and, most of all, calm down before starting back with an armload of wood. She knocked on the cabin door, not wanting to intrude or steal wood. When there was no response, she tried opening it. The place was locked and empty, just like all the others. She wondered if the majority of campers had had enough warning to make it to the canyon rim before the storm hit, although a few cabins still seemed to be occupied.

Where is everyone?

She felt like the lone survivor on a deserted island. Karinne unsuccessfully tried the front windows, but had more luck with a side window. She popped out the screen and crawled in. The sheltered air of the cabin felt stale and almost as cold inside as out. The dry, seasoned wood piled beside the hearth should have made her feel a little better, but didn't. She didn't even have the ambition to start a fire. She sat on the rock hearth, dripping wet.

Karinne lifted the phone—astonished at getting an actual signal. She found Margot's cabin number on the phone sheet posted. Karinne remembered those awful days when she'd waited and waited for a phone call as a child, a call saying Margot was safe. The call that never came.

I'm not her. I'll let everyone know I'm okay.

The phone rang twice before Anita picked up. "Karinne?"

"Anita? It's me," Karinne said immediately.

"Where are you?" Anita asked.

"Fox-5."

"That far?"

"I was looking for dry wood. I'll head back as soon as I get warmed up."

Max's voice replaced Anita's. "Stay where you are. Jon's missing."

"*What?* I'll meet you and start looking."

"No, we'll meet you. We think he went after you and is walking your way. In this mud he'll be able to track you easily enough if you stay put. You'll see him before we will. Stay at the cabin in case he shows up. Light a fire if you can."

"Call me if you find him first, okay?" Karinne begged.

"Got it."

Karinne hung up the phone, her clothes soaked and adding to the puddles on the dull wood floor.

Thank God I called, she thought. She opened the door and stepped outside, back into the rain. It appeared that Jon was as unpredictable as his mother.

Chapter Fifteen

Jon Lazar trudged furiously through the rain, easily following Karinne's deep footprints in the muddy trail. He could barely see the next cabin up ahead, but he wouldn't lose the path. Jon knew how to keep himself safe in isolated terrain. His absent father didn't baby him; he'd instructed him well in the rugged oil camps in raw country. But Jon had never learned to sleep through storms. He'd heard every word Max, Karinne, Cory and his mother had said.

Mom didn't tell Dad everything about Karinne, Jon thought angrily. *Or me. No wonder Dad's not here.*

The three of them always vacationed together. The dreaded "divorce" had been Jon's first fear at the news that his father would not be joining them in the Grand Canyon. Ordinarily a very honest child, he'd secretly started reading his mother's email. He realized his mother was making electronic travel reservations, taking him away from his father. That disturbed him even more, enough to prompt him to read his mother's computer journal. She'd used the same password as far back as he could remember: *shutterbug.*

That was when he learned his parents weren't legally married, that it was all a pretense. Jon had always known he had a sister named Karinne—that was no secret—but he hadn't understood why Margot had never allowed them to meet.

I do now. Mom's still married to Karinne's dad.

Greatly disturbed, Jon had begun reviewing every internet site Margot had "hit" on their home computer. They were all kidney donor sites. The computer work had been easy. He knew how to access the internet. When he was out of school and in the middle of nowhere, the laptop was Jon's entertainment and his connection to his father.

Jon was angry, angrier than he'd ever been in his life. The legal status of his parents' "marriage" paled beside his mother's present behavior. He understood that he had kidney problems, but he didn't know he needed a transplant, or that his mother planned to involve his long-lost sister in this. Margot had still taken him away from his father without Stephan's consent. Worse…*Mom's begging.*

He'd seen beggars in Central America pitifully gathered outside the guarded entrances to oil fields—women, old men, babies who could barely walk, crying for food, water, money. Honor and morals were often sacrificed for a longer life. His father had taught Jon that beggars must be pitied. Except for death, they had no other choice.

But his mother was worse than any beggar.

Beggars could have honor. Leeches didn't. Jon knew about those kinds of people, too. They were the dishonorable opportunists who stole from everyone, even the beggars. Was his mother one of them? In his emails, Jon's father had asked Margot to wait until he returned from the field, yet Margot had taken Jon on a plane and made sure he'd had no further access to her computer.

I don't want Karinne's kidney. I don't even need it right now. I'll get one later. After hearing Max and his mother's conversation, he'd left the cabin. Jon slogged through more puddles. He had to find Karinne—explain how he had nothing to do with Margot's disgraceful behavior. He never begged or lied or pretended, the way his mother had.

He'd find his sister and tell her he wasn't like that. Then, with or without his mother's help, he was going home.

Cabin Fox-5

OUTSIDE ON THE SHELTERED porch, Karinne peered through the rain for any sign of Jon. She was torn with fear for the boy and worry over her argument with Max. He had a point. He always had to step back whenever any of Karinne's family demanded her help. Her father refused to sell the huge home that was too much for him to keep up. Jeff swore vehemently that assisted living communities were for "senior citizens with one foot in the grave," not for him.

Margot expected her to put everything else aside for a stranger Karinne had never met, didn't even know about. Not once had Margot spent any time with Karinne for *Karinne's* sake. All their conversations dealt with Margot's agenda—curing her son.

Karinne realized that her fantasy reunion with her mother would never, ever come true. Regardless of Karinne's age, job and education, she hadn't really gone beyond the day Margot disappeared. She'd stayed frozen, deep inside. Cameras and viewfinders and lenses added a comfortable distance between her and the world. No wonder Max felt she was slipping away from him. She'd never really connected with him.

Her future seemed dismal. She saw the shadow of the canyon's huge wall filtered through the rain—dark and distorted, it reinforced her belief. Even Margot had finally come out into the light. When would it be her turn and Max's?

"Karinne!"

Who had just called her name?

Karinne backtracked toward her mother's cabin. The depth of the water increased as it followed the trail's downward contour, and after passing just one cabin, Karinne found herself wading up to her shins. By the second cabin the water was up to her knees. Her jeans sucked it up like a wick and sent chilly goose bumps down her spine. Karinne lifted her head against the wind, squinting, she peered into the rain.

"Jon? Is that you?"

Cabin Bear-3

SHELTERED FROM the pouring rain, Max reached for his jacket. "Ladies, babysit the phone," he said.

"Wait for me." Cory grabbed his own jacket.

"I'm coming, too. I've got to find Jon and Karinne," Margot insisted. She yanked open the front door and gasped.

The front steps were under the water, which seeped ominously over the landing toward the door.

"Everyone, get your packs," Max ordered, his voice urgent. "We've got to get to higher ground. *Now.*"

Cory joined Max on the porch, just as Max shed his own pack and passed it to his brother.

"Max, what are you doing?"

"I'm going to look for Jon, check on Karinne, then try for the raft while I still can. First, let's get the women up on the roof."

Max didn't bother with details. Monsoons caused flash flooding; water levels could rise a foot a minute—or faster. He gauged the distance from the porch to the slanted roof.

In the background, some of the other campers had emerged to climb onto their own roofs.

"*I'll* get the raft while you check on Jon and Karinne," Cory said. "Let's split the workload."

"Stay with your wife and Margot. I'll go."

Cory spoke in a voice full of emotion. "God, Max…"

Max hugged Cory back, deeply affected. The two brothers broke apart as Cory added, "If you don't come back…"

Cory picked up the plastic five-gallon water jug, emptied most of it out, recapped the lip and shoved it at Max.

"Here, take this. It'll work as a flotation device."

"Thanks."

"And next trip, we keep the damn life jackets *with* us."

"You bet."

"Bon voyage."

Max descended the covered steps and waded into the water as the women came out of the cabin.

"Max is going after the raft," Cory announced.

"But what about Jon and Karinne?" Margot asked.

"Max will get them—and us—in the raft."

"I'm going with him," Margot said defiantly.

Cory grabbed Margot's wrist. "Stay here!"

"Let me go." Margot struggled, trying to yank free.

"No! Max has enough on his hands."

"I don't have to listen to Max."

"True," Cory said. "But you have to listen to *me*."

Cabin Fox-5

KARINNE SPOTTED Jon in cold water up to his waist. Fortunately, the cabin she was in stood on a higher rise than most of the others. She reached for Jon's hand and pulled him onto higher ground.

"What in the world are you doing here?" Karinne asked.

"I wanted to see you."

"By yourself? Are you alone? Where's everyone else?"

"Back at Mom's cabin. They didn't even notice I left," Jon said proudly.

"What were you *thinking?*" In the shallower water, Karinne guided Jon toward the unlocked cabin door. "Mom's gotta be sick with worry."

"You left, too," Jon reminded her.

"I phoned in."

"You still left."

"No, I was looking for wood."

"Well, I was looking for you."

"I can't believe I'm having an argument with you in the water. Your health's bad enough as it is!" Together they waded up onto the porch. "Get in the house," Karinne said. "I'll call the cabin."

"Wait." Jon grabbed at Karinne's sleeve. "It's about Mom."

"Mom?" Karinne repeated.

"And me. She wants your help, but I don't."

"What do you mean?"

"Being a kidney donor. It was Mom's idea, not mine. She didn't ask me. She should have."

Karinne went down on one knee, her face level with Jon's. "That's why you came looking for me?"

"Yes. I had to tell you. Dad doesn't know we're here. I don't want your kidney. I'll go on the donor list. Mom should've put me on it."

"I don't mind helping you, sweetheart...if I can." Karinne hugged him. "Now I have to call her."

Karinne lifted the receiver, but this time, the signal was gone. She tried again, and again.

"What's wrong?"

"It's dead. Great." She slammed the receiver back in its cradle.

"We can hike back," Jon said.

"No, it's too deep."

"But I can swim…."

"Be quiet and let me think, please."

Karinne reviewed their options. The phones were out, the life jackets were in the raft and the raft was moored at the dock. The raft was too valuable to abandon. She didn't know if Max or Cory could reach the dock from Margot's lower location, but Karinne was not only on higher land, she was closer.

"Up on the roof, kiddo." Karinne took Jon's hand and led him out the door.

"In the rain?"

"You won't melt. Use the railing. I'll give you a boost."

Jon wiped his face. "What about you?"

"I have to get the raft. You're staying."

"No."

"Please," she begged. "It's safer if I come back for you."

"You're not my boss!"

True. She needed to inject authority into her voice. Karinne narrowed her eyes as the water crept upward. Something inside her—anger? determination?—flamed. She felt like a forged red-hot piece of hammered metal—waiting to be thrust into the icy rain. She and Jon were both in danger. Would she shatter into brittle, weak shards—or become strong, tempered steel?

"Get over here," she ordered. *"Now."*

Jon remained in place by the open door.

"I'm your sister, and you'll listen to me! Climb up if you want to live. Stay here, and you die. You've got till the count of three. *One.*"

Jon stared at her.

"The waters are rising! You're slowing me down. I can't take you with me, and I won't go unless I know you're safe." Karinne pulled him toward the railing. *"Two."*

"I want Dad," Jon whispered.

"What about our mother? She'll drown without the raft—we all will. What's it going to be, Jon? Time's up. *Three.*"

Jon scrambled upward, his sneakers on the porch railing. Karinne easily boosted him up, then followed. On the porch roof, she watched incredulously as the waters quickly covered the railing. She didn't waste any more time looking.

"Jon, watch me. Do this if the water gets any higher." She took off her boots and dropped her jeans, her one-piece swimsuit now covered only by a blouse.

"I'm making a life preserver. Watch carefully."

Karinne tied the end of her jeans legs in a large knot. She slung the jeans above her head and circled them like a revolving door, inflating them as best she could. Next she rolled up the waist of the jeans, trapping the air inside.

"Make sure your jeans are wet first. Hold the waistband closed with your fingers, like this."

Jon nodded. The water was now covering the porch railing.

"Then tuck a pants leg under each arm. Like this. See? If the water comes higher than the roof, inflate your jeans— you'll have to do it more than once—and concentrate on breathing. I'll be back soon. Hold on to the chimney so you don't drift."

"How long?"

"I don't know. But if any rescuers come while I'm gone, go with them. They might show up once the floodwaters recede."

"You'll come back here first?"

"I hope so. Get your shoes off and stay on this highest part of the roof. Keep your shoes if you can. Don't wait until the last minute to take off your jeans, okay?"

Jon nodded again.

"Okay, then. Stay calm, and I'll let you steer the raft when I get back."

"Promise?"

"Hey, I'm your sister! Would I lie?"

She lifted her arms to inflate her jeans.

"I've never driven a boat before," Jon said, excited.

"Raft," Karinne corrected. *And neither have I.*

She gave Jon a cheerful thumbs-up, watched the water flow even with the porch roof and jumped.

Chapter Sixteen

Cabin Bear-3

Margot huddled on her cabin's porch roof, peering through the binoculars, keeping track of Max's progress. Margot had lost the fight to go after Max when water had started streaming into the cabin. She'd let Cory and Anita help her onto the roof with a minimum of gear. Margot vaguely remembered experiencing a panic attack until Cory had found the binoculars, spotted Max and shoved them into her hands.

"Keep watching him," Cory had said. "He'll find the others, so don't lose sight." Margot now held the binoculars so tightly her fingers were white, the bright blue of Max's floating five-gallon water jug easy to track. Cory and Anita remained below to remove the front cabin door from the hinges.

"Just in case we need a makeshift raft," Cory murmured. He reached for the multipurpose knife he always carried in his pocket and flipped out the small screwdriver blade.

"You sure the door will float?" Anita asked as Cory wedged the blade into the upper pins of the door's three hinges.

"It's pine, and it's painted," Cory said. "It'll float."

He wiggled, pounded, then pulled the highest pin free

and tossed it. Next he lined up the screwdriver blade in the thin gap between the door and the middle hinge pin.

"Will it float with three people and packs, too? Should we lighten them?" Anita asked.

"We might have to leave them here, but we need to get this door free and secured first." The middle pin popped up and out. Anita held the door handle.

"One more."

Anita stabilized the door. Cory squatted, water on the porch lapping at his ankles. The pin suddenly released, and despite Anita's grasp, the door arced toward the window, its pointed corner shattering glass.

Anita jumped at the sound. "It's broken."

"They can take it out of my taxes," Cory said without missing a beat as he joined Anita and pulled the door free of the window frame.

"Watch out, I'm letting it fall," Cory warned.

The door floated easily in the rising water. He unscrewed the doorknob and totally removed it, then slipped off his belt and buckled the leather in a loop through the doorknob hole. By now the water on the porch was up to his knees. Other rooftop inhabitants across the trail watched the proceedings, but stayed where they were. Cory concentrated on his task.

"Anita, go on the roof. I need your belt. Yours, too, Margot." Cory locked his fingers together to make a step for Anita's foot. "Up you go."

"That door's not going to hold all the packs," Margot said from atop the porch roof. The door, while buoyant, was thin, not the thicker width used in snow country. She slid her belt out from her pant loops.

"No, but it'll hold us. Here, take the end while I climb up." Cory passed Anita the three belts. He'd rebuckled all three loops through the knob so they'd have individual handles if they had to abandon the roof. Cory sprang upward off the railing and joined the other two on the cabin roof. The door floated on the water below.

"Toss me the belt," he said to Anita. "I'll hold it now."

She did. "Cory…"

"Hmm?"

"I can't swim."

Cory froze. Even Margot lowered the binoculars.

"That's not funny, Anita."

"I know. My parents don't swim, either. That's why I've never gone rafting with you before."

Cory stared. "Why didn't you ever tell me? I'm your husband. I could have taught you."

"I should have, but it never came up," Anita said in a shaky voice.

"Doesn't matter." Cory took her cold hand. "I can swim for both of us."

Raft docks

KARINNE HAD BEEN half swimming, half wading to the dock, until only a final section of deep water separated her from the raft. She'd kept to the higher land and was almost there. Gauging the distance between her present location and the dock, she could see the bright yellow of the raft through the rain. Although the dock itself was barely visible, it wasn't underwater yet. Already the water was up to her hips, and the closer she got to the Colorado, the more she worried.

Let Jon be okay until I get back… And the rest of them… Max, Cory, Anita, her mother. Karinne slipped, losing her footing. She couldn't pick herself up; she had to swim. At any other time she'd feel confident swimming the short distance, but this was no gentle lake. The floodwaters tugged on the raft like a wild thing, yanking at the line as the river rushed by. From her position she could see that some canoes had overturned, and a small trolling motor rowboat was swamped. The larger, more powerful ranger boat was gone.

If she angled her swim and tacked diagonally, she'd have a better chance of success. But her jeans were deflating. Karinne reinflated them. She tucked a jean leg under each arm, praying her makeshift life preserver would last. She didn't waste her energy trying to escape the current. She concentrated on keeping her angle true to the dock.

She floated and kicked closer, but started drifting off course. Her inflated pants were leaking air again. Then the shoreline current ripped away her sagging jeans. Karinne didn't panic. She straightened her body into a modified crawl, using her legs to kick. She was maybe an Olympic-pool length away. If she focused on her breathing and conserved her strength, she should reach the dock.

As soon as she did, Karinne pushed wet hair off her face and pulled herself into the raft. As she threw herself over the side, the last of her buttons popped. Her shirt gaped open. She didn't notice. All she could do was lie on the raft floor, panting for breath. The raft bobbed and jerked, its figure-eight line secured to the two-pronged dock cleat. Max usually started the boat and Cory would toss the line free from the dock and hop in. But mounted engines had a safety cut-off, a dead man's switch. If she started it and released the tiller to undo the line, the engine would automatically stop. If she released the line before the engine started, the raft could get sucked into the Colorado instead of toward the cabins.

What to do?

Engine first, line second, she decided. The wind tore at her clothes. Karinne took off her boots and dropped her jeans, her swimsuit covered by her shirt. She crawled on her hands and knees toward the engine mount in the bouncing raft.

I'll fire it up. How hard can it be? She'd never piloted before, but this wasn't exactly an aircraft carrier. She'd always been observant.

I'm a photographer, for heaven's sake! She'd watched Max and Cory start the engine all week—a simple two-stroke with a pull ignition.

It's like starting a lawn mower. She mentally reviewed the speed indicator guide on the tiller. The controller grip on the outboard twisted clockwise and counterclockwise for greater or lesser speeds.

She spotted the pull-cord ignition. She kept one arm on the raft rope, and yanked with the other. Her efforts were laughable. She couldn't even pull out the full length of the cord. The boat moved with her momentum, not the cord.

Gotta brace myself, then pull. She did, placing her bare feet against the inflatable sides, facing the engine, then pulled the rope again, using both hands. The engine putt-putted once and stopped.

Be patient. Come on, start!

This time she smelled gas. She hadn't yet pulled the cord its full length.

I flooded the engine.

Karinne released the ignition pull, salvaged the spare binoculars and threw the strap over her neck. She put on a life jacket and retrieved the bail bucket, then began bailing water out of the raft, panting from exertion and fear.

How long do I have to wait? If she tried too soon, she'd flood the engine more. And if she hesitated too long, the people waiting for her at the cabins could drown.

Karinne reached for the pull-start line, braced her feet

again and yanked with every ounce of strength she had, ripping the cord from the engine casing.

Lightning cracked high above, echoing through the canyon walls, its flash illuminating the pull cord—disconnected from the engine—dangling like a dead rattlesnake in her hand. The dead man's switch had killed all power.

Karinne stared at the useless ignition cord and the docked line, then screamed in pure rage.

This is truly the vacation from hell!

Cabin Bear-3

THERE, ON THE CABIN roof, near the chimney, the three adults silently waited and watched the water rise. As it rapidly flooded over the porch roof and crept toward the cabin roof's apex, Cory pulled Anita and Margot higher. All three held on to the belts connecting them to their door raft. Binoculars hanging from her neck, Margot swallowed hard as the water crept closer. There wasn't much of the roof above water. She'd lost sight of Max long ago.

"Okay, ladies," Cory announced. "All aboard that's going aboard."

Anita's eyes were wide and round, Margot's hands shook, but Cory didn't hesitate. He maneuvered the door so he lay belly-down in the middle, the top and bottom of the door like wings on either side, the doorknob hole above his head. He helped Anita lower herself to his right as Margot took the left.

"Hold on tight, and keep your hands and feet inside the vehicle at all times," Cory joked. "It's going to be a bumpy ride."

The water rose higher, taking the door out and away from the submerged cabin, leaving only the roof ridge and the top of the chimney behind. The water churned and roiled with debris as it continued to rise. Steering proved impossible, and cottonwood tops loomed dangerously above the water.

"Everyone, kick harder!" Cory yelled to Margot, one arm around Anita, the other holding his strap.

"I am kicking!" Margot yelled back.

"We're gonna hit the tree!" Anita said.

Seconds later the door jammed among the higher branches of a tall cottonwood, and wedged in tight. The wood, parallel to the waterline, didn't budge.

Anita shivered. "At least we aren't drifting anymore."

"Now what?" Margot asked.

"Sit up, heads above the water. Grab a branch and don't let go," he warned Anita as he gave her a helpful push so she could sit. Her legs dangled directly in the water.

"We're stuck, aren't we?" Margot said.

"Thanks for pointing that out, Mrs. C," Cory replied with more than a little sarcasm as he rubbed his hands up and down Anita's arms. "You still have the binocs?"

Margot immediately swung the binoculars up from her neck to her eyes.

"Can you see anyone?" Anita asked, her teeth chattering.

"No, we're too low," Margot said.

"We're higher than the cabins," Cory said. "We can climb even higher if we have to. And the lower branches should protect us from debris."

The three of them silently studied the chimneys of the cabins, the only structural features still visible above water. Cory actually stood on the door.

"Give me those binoculars," he said. "Maybe I can see something standing up."

"I'll do it." Margot got up to stand on the door herself, the rain running into the furrows on her forehead and around the rubber eyepieces.

"Stop moving the door, Margot!" Anita pleaded. "Sit d—"

Anita never finished her sentence. The water surged, shaking the tree and the door. Margot lost her grip and splashed into the water, while Cory and Anita remained on the door. Margot didn't surface.

"Margot!" Anita yelled.

"Where'd she go?" Cory searched frantically amid the branches. He shoved his belt loop into Anita's hand.

"I don't know! I didn't see!"

Anita pointed to the far end of the door. "Over there!"

Cory released Anita, wrapped his fingers around the tree branches, then pulled his body down and deliberately submerged himself in the dark waters.

Chapter Seventeen

Cabin Fox-5

Max finally reached Karinne's cabin. He was agonizingly cold, but his progress had been rapid enough with the current. The water rose ever higher, tearing off the porches and roofs in big chunks that immediately sank, or smaller pieces that floated in the water. He wondered how much time he had before the cabins themselves collapsed under the weight of the water. The five-gallon jug was effective as a float, but it wouldn't protect him from floating debris.

Before Max's gaze focused on the child, Jon yelled out his name.

"Jon? You okay?" Max yelled back.

"Yes!"

Carefully avoiding floating branches, Max kicked over to the ridgepole where the boy stood. Even the cabin's rock-and-cement chimney had begun to crumble, leaving a jagged outline at the waterline. The ridgepole would soon be submerged, as well. Jon hugged the chimney tightly, his jeans floating limply around his waist.

"Where's Karinne?" Max asked, the air against his soaked body feeling even colder than the water.

"She went for the raft."

The chill spreading through his body had nothing to do with the temperature. "When?"

"A while ago. When the water was lower. I hope she's okay. Are you going out there?"

"No. I can't make the dock in this current."

The whole foundation of the cabin beneath them shook. Jon grabbed at the chimney, but it fell away in pieces. Max clutched Jon's arm just as the upper half of the chimney swayed. They both scooted to the opposite side of the roof and Jon's pants sank with the chimney rocks.

"My jeans!" Jon gasped. He started to move toward the chimney, but Max reeled him back.

"Here," Max said. He shoved the water jug's plastic handle toward Jon. "Use this."

As he took it, Jon studied Max, who wore hiking shorts and a T-shirt.

"What about you?"

"I'll tread water until I find something else." Max anchored his bare feet against the submerged cabin roof shingles.

"There isn't anything," Jon said.

"Then we'll wait for something to float by—the raft, if we're lucky. With Karinne on it."

"What if she's late?"

"We'll tag-team."

"What?"

"Take turns floating and treading water. You float first. Then we switch."

"No, you first. You're tired," Jon said.

"Stop arguing, kid."

The whole cabin suddenly swayed beneath them.

"You hold the float. I'll swim. Now!" Max said.

That was when the cabin beneath them collapsed and burst apart in the water.

The top bar of the porch ripped through the water. It whipped hard against Jon's leg, hitting with a force that would've shattered bone had the water not cushioned the impact. Jon gasped in pain, and swallowed a mouthful of water as the blow separated him from Max—and from the buoy. Max didn't see the injury, but immediately threw one arm across the boy's chest and held Jon's head high; as he did, he reached for and regained the floating container.

Max tread water, desperately keeping Jon's head above the water as the boy choked for breath. Jon had both arms on the float, and only one leg to kick with.

"Are you okay?"

"My leg hurts," Jon gasped.

"Can you move it?"

"Some."

There was no way they could take turns treading water now. Max held on to the jug handle to keep Jon from being swept away. The two of them, human cargo, awkwardly bobbed and drifted amid the wreckage with other desperate campers.

Karinne, where are you?

CORY FOLLOWED the tree, going down legs first, his eyes useless in the clay-filled water. Holding his breath, he used his feet like feelers, probing in all directions while hugging the tree with his arms. He found nothing and was forced to surface for air. He looked for Anita, who was still on the door. He heard her calling Margot's name as he ducked under again. Margot couldn't have floated away; she'd fallen up-current, so the underwater branches of the tree should have snagged her.

He felt a line stretch taut across his foot. *The binocular strap!* Cory didn't resurface, afraid he wouldn't be able to pinpoint the location again. Still submerged, he released the tree, spun head down into the water and followed the strap a little farther, his hand ending up at Margot's head. He pushed her hard, his lungs bursting as he sprang upward off the branches, straining—afraid he wouldn't make the surface with her, afraid to surface without her. Suddenly, Margot broke free, and Cory shot upward, Margot floating with him.

Before her head cleared the water, Anita reached for Cory and pulled the two of them toward her.

"She's not breathing." Cory started coughing, his lungs searing with pain as he took in fresh air. Anita dragged him onto the door, then began resuscitation procedures on Margot while Cory collapsed faceup, hyperventilating and praying Anita could breathe life back into Margot.

KARINNE GROANED with effort as she lifted the small but heavy trolling motor and battery from the tiny rowboat and dumped it on the dock. She managed to drop Max's larger gas motor from its mounts. She didn't even try to save it. The engine sank quickly, resting beneath the dock on the bed of dark red clay. Then she scrambled back onto the dock, manhandled the rowboat's electric motor and battery onto Max's raft and used the hand clamps to reposition it.

The motor looked pitifully small compared to the one she'd scuttled, but it was all she could lift. At least the electric motor turned on with a switch, no keys or pull start required.

Karinne flipped the switch. Nothing. She primed the engine once and cautiously tried again. *Success!* As long as the marine battery had enough juice, she was in business.

Karinne tossed off the line and motored the raft away from the dock. The craft handled clumsily as she over-steered with the troller. She felt like an inexperienced young teen behind the wheel of a car for the very first time—and on a speeding highway with no helpful instructor beside her. Despite her ignorance of boating, the chill of the water and, most of all, her fear for the others, she appreciated the power of nature at its rawest. She thought of Powell, who'd had only one arm to steer with. If he could do it, she could, too—at least long enough to get to Max.

But Powell had navigational skills. Karinne had none. As she came within view of what had once been the cabins, her heart sank. Her only landmarks were half-destroyed chimney tops and the tops of partially submerged cottonwoods. She had to find the others.

Where do I start looking?

CORY WORKED on chest compressions as Anita continued to breathe into the unconscious woman's mouth.

"She's not breathing yet!"

"Switch!" he ordered. He cleaned out Margot's mouth and nose a second time and pushed hard breaths into the woman's lungs.

"I've got a pulse," Anita said thankfully.

Cory couldn't celebrate. Margot remained unconscious, eyes closed. She finally coughed and started breathing on her own, but she was limp, not responding to her name.

"Roll her on her side," Anita said. "I'll dry her off."

Cory unbuttoned his shirt. Anita balled it up and wrung it out to sponge off Margot's face.

"She still breathing okay?" Cory asked. "How's her pulse?"

"Good, but I wish she'd wake up," Anita said. "We're down to one swimmer now—you. Where's Max? Do you think he made it to the raft?"

"I don't know." Cory took his shirt back, but didn't have the energy to put it on. "He'd better show up soon. We're running out of time."

THE RAIN ENDED monsoon-style—just as abruptly as it had started, with almost no transitional phase from pouring to stopping. The light was improved, too, as Karinne piloted the raft among the remains of cottonwood trees and chimneys. Unfortunately, the floodwaters didn't disappear as quickly as they'd risen. That could take days.

"Anyone there?" she yelled again and again. Her throat ached from overuse, but she kept yelling the question, calling out names. Her voice cracked, temporarily gone. She brought her fingers to her lips and whistled....

And, incredibly, she heard a responding whistle.

"Max?" she shouted.

"Karinne!" a voice shouted back. "It's Cory!"

Karinne spotted him. He waved a shirt in the air. "Over here!"

It *was* Cory. And Anita. And...who else? Karinne wasn't close enough to see, nor could she maneuver over to the trees.

"Stay put." Cory jumped into the water and swam toward the raft, replacing Karinne at the tiller. He took the raft much closer, close enough for Karinne to see Anita, and her mother's motionless body.

"What happened?" Karinne asked, her heart in her throat. "What's wrong with Mom? Where's Max?"

"Max went after Jon. Margot went under," Cory said.

"She's not—"

"She's breathing, but still out of it. It'll take both of us to load her into the raft," Cory said.

"Anita, you okay?" Karinne studied Anita frantically.

"I'm fine."

"Except my wife can't swim."

"What?"

"It's true," Anita said.

"I've got life jackets." Karinne grabbed two and rolled overboard with them.

Cory edged the raft a little nearer. "I can't get any closer—not with this motor. Where's ours?"

"Broken," Karinne said, reaching the door. She gasped aloud, shocked at the sight of her mother's limp body. Karinne passed Anita a life jacket.

"Cory pulled her out of the water. She wasn't breathing when he brought her up," Anita said bluntly.

"Oh, God."

Anita helped Karinne put a life jacket on Margot.

"It's okay, Mom," Karinne said to the unmoving figure. "We're getting out of here."

Soon the three women were in the raft. Karinne held Margot, her mother's head motionless on her lap.

"Give me a paddle," Anita told Cory.

Cory tossed her one from the bottom of the boat.

"We're making progress," he said encouragingly.

"Two more passengers and we're home free," Anita added.

Karinne settled her mother more carefully in her lap and reached for the other paddle. "We aren't there yet. We have to find Jon and Max."

MAX KEPT HIS ARMS linked under Jon's arms, the boy's back against Max's chest. Max's muscles were cramped with the cold. He suspected the water had long since siphoned away much of Jon's body heat, as it had his. The boy's leg had to be throbbing from its lashing by the rail, and his strength was fading. Max's own energy was severely taxed. He'd let the water take them where it wanted, conserving his strength, kicking only when dangerous flotsam threatened them.

"You okay?" he asked Jon, repeating the conversation

they'd been having for the past hour, both of them saying the same words. "How's your leg?"

"Fine. Where's the raft?"

"Maybe in another ten minutes."

This time, Jon's response varied from the script.

"You said that before..." His weak voice sounded impatient. "Check your watch."

Max carefully angled his wrist. The digital dial had gone blank. "It's broken."

"Why didn't you buy a waterproof one?"

"I did," Max said ruefully. "I guess it just died."

"Are *we* gonna die?"

"No."

"Is anyone gonna find us?" Jon asked. His voice trembled, not from cold or pain, but from fear.

"They'll be here soon."

"Are you sure?"

Max cuddled the boy closer. Jon's limbs felt stiff, wooden. So did his. "We just have to wait a few more minutes."

"I wish I had a cell phone." Jon sighed.

"Won't work here. They don't make waterproof ones, anyway, do they?"

"They do, too! Go online and look."

"Tell you what," Max promised. "When we get out of here, I'll buy you a cell phone. Waterproof."

"Mom won't let you."

"Yes, she will. I'm an old friend of Karinne's. I'm practically family."

"Then *you* ask Mom," Jon said.

"I will...when we see her."

"Soon."

Max managed to smile, despite failing strength and the taste of dirty water. "Soon," he agreed.

KARINNE CONTINUED to steer, her eyes scanning the waters. She couldn't lose Max. He was her heart, her soul, her life. Somehow she'd repair the rift between them—but first, she had to find him. And Jon, the brother she'd never known. She couldn't lose him. She'd just found him.

"Where can he be?" Anita asked anxiously.

"There!" Cory sang out. "I see them! Max!"

Cory directed the raft toward them as Karinne and Anita stowed their paddles. Max shoved Jon toward the waiting arms above him. He was numb from the cold. He couldn't feel his fingers as he pushed Jon upward into the raft. Anita and Margot, who'd regained consciousness, took the boy as Cory and Karinne carefully pulled Max in without swamping the craft. Cory dropped the tiller to help, but Karinne reached Max first.

HE FELT HER ARMS around him as he was half pulled, half rolled over the edge of the raft. He fell into Karinne's lap—limp, spent, eyes closed against the muck. Karinne tenderly wiped his face with gentle fingers. He'd never felt so tired. He'd never felt so good, either.

The others in the boat shot out rapid-fire questions about Max's and Jon's welfare. Max couldn't make sense of any of the words, but even with his eyes shut, he registered Karinne's soft voice. She was the one person not shouting his name over and over, Cory loudest of all, but only Karinne's presence registered.

"Open your eyes, Max," Cory insisted.

"Max…Max…Max…" Everyone shouted his name.

"Quiet, everyone!" someone ordered.

Karinne? To Max's amazement, everyone obeyed the command.

"Give him some air. Let him catch his breath." Karinne's voice, sweet and low, rang with love.

"Max, listen to me. We're all here. Every one of us. Help will be here soon. The storm's over."

He felt Karinne wrap herself more closely around him, his head tucked under her chin. Max sighed, soaking up her love. He still couldn't talk, but he was starting to feel warm again....

"You look better," she said, smoothing his wet hair.

"I feel better."

"Just relax for now, okay?"

Relax? Max couldn't remember lowering his guard, ever. He hadn't allowed himself a break. He hadn't dared. His whole life he'd been the leader, and the leader never rested—until now. Karinne was taking charge, taking care of *him*. With Karinne, he could catch his breath. That was all he'd ever needed to make life perfect. A loving woman to share life's load.

He almost lost faith in that strong, kindred soul he'd recognized, but now he wondered if perhaps Karinne *had* remained true to herself, and to him.

"Can you open your eyes?" Karinne asked.

He could move mountains for this woman—with this woman—but only if she could stand on her own two feet. He opened his eyes to her face.

I thought I'd never see you again. He took in a deep breath, but could only gasp out, "You're here...."

"Of course I'm here." Karinne smiled, her love shining. She brought one of his hands to her lips, kissed his palm and held it against her cheek. "I told you I'd never let go of you."

"You're just saying that...because I went missing."

"Yes. And no." She kissed his head and hugged him so tightly that once more he couldn't breathe. But this time, he didn't mind. He kept her face in focus as his strength returned.

Max held Karinne's hand, continued to hold it as a helicopter's rotary blades sang high above the Colorado. He sat up with her fingers in his, wishing she still wore his engagement ring, wishing things could be right between them and praying for a future with the only woman he'd ever loved as the approaching sound of rescue reverberated against the walls of the Grand Canyon.

Chapter Eighteen

Karinne concentrated on her driving. She was headed back to Phoenix with Margot, Jon and Max. After their rescue and helicopter flight to the top of the canyon, EMTs had checked everyone out. No one showed lasting effects of the ordeal and exposure to the cold, although Jon had a severely bruised leg and had been ordered to stay off it for a few days. Margot's submersion underwater and the near-loss of both her children had left her shaky and subdued. Max had simply been exhausted, but that was nothing rest wouldn't cure. A good night's sleep topside had done wonders.

Cory and Anita were staying at the canyon.

"I'm giving you swimming lessons as soon as I can get you to a pool," Cory told his wife. "And you want to join me in the rafting business?"

"I never said I didn't need on-the-job training," she replied. "I am an accountant, after all."

"Don't ever surprise me like that again," Cory said. "I can't take it."

Karinne wanted to go home to Phoenix. As she explained to Margot, "You need to see Dad again, Mom. You two have a lot to talk over." She didn't add, *And divorce papers to sign,* but that was implied.

"I'll go with you," Max had volunteered. And he had. He sat beside her in the front seat, for once not offering to drive. Karinne suspected the ordeal in the water had taken more out of him than he'd admitted, both physically and emotionally.

Margot and Jon dozed in the backseat, still recovering, the long drive to Phoenix giving them time to rest. Max remained awake, but quiet.

"Thanks for coming along with me," Karinne said.

"No problem. I told you I'd see this through to the end."

Her fingers tightened on the steering wheel. "I don't like hearing those words from you."

"What?"

"The end." Karinne kept her eyes on the road. "Although I've realized that change, whether good or bad, is always stressful. But speaking of 'the end,' I've got to end some things in *my* life, Max. The first is my job." She could feel his gaze on her, and flicked him a quick glance before looking out through her windshield again. "I'm tired of living a nomad's life. I have no free time for anyone or anything, not myself, not you. I know it's a little late, but I'm moving up north. I want us to rediscover each other, to be together as a couple—whether we get married or not."

"You sure you wanna give up your job?" Max asked. "You've worked hard to get where you are, Karinne."

"I know. But…I need to. I have money set aside I've never had time to spend, nor have I had time for the people I love. That's why I cling so hard to my father. But my brief visits with him—and with you—aren't enough. And now there's Mom and Jon. I want a regular life—but most of all I want to be with you. I know you think it's probably too late, but it doesn't have to be."

She tried to keep the pleading out of her voice, but she didn't hide the love she felt.

"I did a lot of thinking myself while I was treading

water," Max said. "I was so worried about you…afraid I'd never see you again. I can't believe you went after the raft, Karinne. You swam in a flood, you'd never piloted a raft, yet you went, anyway. You've got courage, more courage than I realized. You're not a child waiting to grow up. I was wrong. You're a woman—a woman any man would be proud to have as his bride."

Karinne blinked the tears from her eyes. "I don't want *any* man. I just want you."

"We'll try again," Max said. "But let's not make any promises. Let's see what's going to happen with Margot and Jon. It's easier to break ties with a job than it is to rock the boat with your family. Jeff isn't going to want to let you go, and I can see him using Margot's reappearance as another reason to hold on to his only daughter. That's what he does, Karinne. It's what he's done ever since Margot ran away. He'll have to deal with the pain of Margot's rejection— something you haven't done, either."

"Just because I haven't said anything doesn't mean I don't feel it," Karinne said, her voice hoarse with emotion. "Of course I'm angry. And sad. And confused. My own mother left me, had another child, loved him, stayed with him and only came back to me because that child's sick. What am I supposed to do, Max? Tell her I hate her as much as I love her?"

"No." He laid his hand softly on her thigh as she drove. "Understand that she's flawed. Understand that you're on the bottom of Margot's list. Know that she looks out for her own interests first—and maybe her son's—and act accordingly."

"And I guess that goes for my father, as well."

"At times, yes. But don't judge them too harshly. Love them all you can. Just stand up and fight for what you want, like they do."

"I know what I want. You," Karinne said quietly. "But I haven't fought for you, not for a long time. Not until yesterday, when I knew I had to get the raft. I couldn't let anything happen to any of the people I care about. I especially couldn't let you down. And I won't," she vowed. "You'll see."

Max said nothing.

Karinne wondered if he really believed her capable of doing what she'd said. She felt certain deep down that she was but, all the same, was glad Max had come with her. The meeting between Margot and Jeff would be a war zone, and there was still the transplant issue to settle for Jon.

The Phoenix sun shone brightly as Karinne pulled off the interstate. She drove toward her apartment, everyone awake now, alert and nervous. Max and Jon were to stay at Karinne's place and have lunch, while Karinne and Margot would continue on to Jeff's house.

"I'll see you later," Karinne said softly, kissing Max on the cheek.

Margot hugged her son, told him to behave and reentered the car with her daughter.

"Are you sure you don't want to have some lunch first?" Karinne asked as she pulled away from the curb.

Margot shook her head. "No, I'm too nervous. Does your father know we're coming?"

"I called him."

"I hope he doesn't have the police waiting for me. Or any other nasty surprises."

"No, Mom. It'll just be the three of us. Or just the two of you, if you'd like privacy."

"I want you there," Margot said. "I imagine we'll need a referee. Your father never had much patience."

"What do you expect?" Karinne asked bluntly. "You walked out on him and me. You faked your own death. Dad isn't going to tamely hold out an olive branch and welcome you with open arms. That would be asking too much."

Margot said nothing during the rest of the drive. Fifteen minutes later Karinne turned into the driveway, parking behind her father's vehicle. She climbed out, gazing at the outside of her childhood home, imagining how her mother would see it. The beige of the Arizona-style stucco walls on either side of the front door. The green of a cactus garden, complete with a rusted iron wagon wheel that broke up the monotone of the beige and added color to the front yard. Various succulents, including aloe plants and agaves, grew at the foot of the walls, and a yellow mailbox added the finishing touch.

"It seems older," Margot whispered, coming up beside her. "Yet still the same."

Karinne didn't respond. She went up to the front door and, for once, didn't enter as she'd been doing all her life. She rang the doorbell and waited for her father to answer. Margot twisted the strap of her purse with both hands, her head bowed.

The door opened. "Hi, Dad," Karinne said. "We're here." The words sounded silly after all the years Margot had been missing.

Jeff stood back and motioned them in. Karinne suddenly realized how old and worn her father looked. The deep lines in his face seemed deeper as he stared at his wife.

"Aren't you going to say hello, Jeff?" Margot asked hesitantly as Jeff closed the door and gestured the two women to the couch.

"Why? You never said goodbye."

Margot flinched at the bitterness in his voice. Karinne curled her fingers around her mother's forearm.

"Max has already filled me in on your actions," Jeff said. "We might as well take care of business first." He crossed the room to his desk, removing a pen and manila envelope from a drawer. "These are the divorce papers. Under the circumstances, there's no alimony. I'm asking for a divorce on the grounds of spousal desertion. Feel free to read them over, but I want them signed before you leave this house."

Margot's face paled, but she took her reading glasses out of her purse and then accepted the papers. After a few minutes, she said, "These seem to be in order."

"Then sign in the appropriate places. They're all marked with Post-its."

Margot's hand trembled just a moment, then she wrote her signature where required. She slid the papers back in the envelope and handed it to Jeff.

"Is there anything you'd like to ask me, Jeff?"

"No. Yes." His eyes blazed. "It's bad enough that you walked out on me. Why did you walk out on our daughter?"

"I never planned to leave her behind," Margot said. "I wanted to take her with me. I had her clothes packed, a passport, a plane ticket for her, everything."

"What stopped you?" Jeff asked.

Margot faced her daughter. "You were at Max and Cory's house. I went to bring you home, and Max lied. Said you weren't there. I looked all over, but finally I couldn't wait any longer. So I left without you."

"My God. You would actually have taken Karinne away from me?"

Margot lifted her chin. "Yes. I'm not proud of it, but yes. I loved her. I didn't want to leave her behind."

"And you would've pretended...what? That my daughter was dead, too?"

Silence. Karinne might have bolted from the couch if

her legs hadn't felt like jelly. "Mom, how could you have done that to Dad? To me?"

"I loved you!"

For the first time, Karinne understood what Max meant when he said love alone wasn't enough. Actions counted, as well, and Margot's actions had destroyed a lot of her husband's and daughter's happiness. If Margot had kidnapped her, Jeff's life would've been ruined forever.

Tears filled Jeff's eyes and ran down his cheeks. He brusquely wiped them away, his fist clenched on the envelope with his divorce papers. Karinne went to him. She wrapped her arm around his shoulders for reassurance.

"Can you forgive me, Jeff?" Margot asked, her own eyes wet. "After all these years?"

"I could have forgiven you for the gambling, for the money, even for staying away without a word. But abandoning our daughter, risking the house—her home—and then showing up again only because of your son? No, Margot, I won't forgive you for that. And if anything happens to Karinne, I'll make sure you spend the rest of your life in jail. After the divorce, I hope I never see you again. I wish you'd stayed dead, Margot. I really do."

Margot broke down entirely. She clutched her purse and rushed to the front door, managing to gulp out, "I'll wait in the car."

"You aren't going after her?" Jeff asked.

"You're the parent who raised me, not her." Karinne hugged her father tightly. "Dad, I'm so sorry."

"Thank God for Max," Jeff whispered, his chin on her shoulder. "If Margot had taken you, if I'd lost you both, I don't know what I would have done. Gone crazy. Why didn't she tell me about the gambling?"

"I don't know, Dad."

"I would've been angry, but the three of us could still have had a future. You would've had a mother."

Karinne gently broke away from him and pulled the envelope out of his hand to place on the desk. All this drama couldn't be good for his heart. She sat down on the couch again and took both his hands in hers.

"I wish I could stay with you right now, but I'll come back later."

"Stay as long as you want. Margot can sit in the damn car and wait."

"Max and Jon are at my apartment. I thought I'd leave Margot and Jon there, and Max and I could come back here."

Her father nodded. "He's a good man. Don't let him get away, Karinne."

"I don't intend to. Are you going to be all right while I'm gone? Is there anyone you want me to call?"

"No, I'll be fine."

"You sure?" Karinne suspected her father needed a few minutes alone.

"Uh-huh. Drive carefully," he warned, giving her a kiss on the cheek.

"I'll pick us up some dinner. Chicken okay?"

"Fine."

"I love you, Dad," she said, her eyes teary again. "Later."

Margot was still crying when Karinne got back in her car. Karinne said nothing. She checked her cell phone—no messages from Max—and started the car. She carefully looked for traffic, then pulled out into the street. Margot didn't settle down until about three miles later, when she swiped at her eyes and nose one last time, then put the tissue back inside her purse. Karinne didn't feel sympathetic. All in all, she felt her mother had gotten off rather lightly.

"So do you think your father will have me jailed for insurance fraud?" Margot asked.

"I don't think that's up to Dad. It's up to the insurance company you defrauded."

"Maybe Jon and I should go back to Mexico. You can come with us and be tested for donor status there. Surely you can get some time off work."

Karinne braked for a red light and faced her mother. "I'm not going to Mexico. I'm not going anywhere that takes me away from Max."

"But if I get arrested…"

Legally, it's what you deserve, she thought.

"And what about Jon? He needs a transplant!"

"So you've told me, Mother."

"What happened to *Mom?* What about your brother?"

"I've agreed to be tested for donor compatibility, and I will. Here. In Phoenix."

"And you'll give Jon your kidney if he needs it?"

She shook her head, then pressed the gas as the light changed to green. "I'll consider giving Jon my kidney, depending on the circumstances."

"What?"

"You never told me if you placed Jon on the list. Max said to ask."

Margot didn't deny it. "Everyone knows a family donor is better than a stranger donor."

"But, Mom, you didn't even try."

"There's still a chance you're compatible."

"As I've said, I'm willing to step in if I'm a match and no one else is, when—if—he ever reaches the critical stage. But you need to explore all other options first."

"Your father put you up to this, didn't he? And Max!"

"No. But Max and Dad have to be my first priority. Especially Max. Have you told Jon he could live a long life without my help? Does his father know?"

"Stephan knows Jon's sick, but—"

"Did he approve of your coming to me? Answer the question, Mother."

"This was all my idea."

"Does he even know you're here?"

Margot flushed. "He's working. I could hardly ask him to drop everything, could I?"

"No, but you asked me."

"Jon's my son! You're my daughter!"

"I haven't been your daughter for a long time, Mother. What I said stands. Put Jon on the donor list."

"But he might only have months!" Margot insisted.

"And he might have a lot longer. Jon's traveled cross-country. He's traveled, ridden mules, hiked. I believe you lied to me about how sick he really is."

"Months, years, who knows? Doctors aren't perfect! I can't take that chance."

"Max warned me," Karinne murmured. "I should have listened. He was right."

"Darling…"

"Enough." Karinne lifted her head and met her mother's gaze head-on. "*If* Jon's health starts to fail before they find him a match, then come to me."

Margot rummaged inside her purse for a tissue and started crying again. "You want revenge because I left you."

"No, Mom."

"I swear, I wanted to take you with me!"

Thank God you didn't. Dad was right. Thank God Max stopped her. I would never have had a normal life.

Back at Karinne's apartment, Max told her Jeff had called and decided he didn't want company after all. Margot, with

Jon in tow, elected to go to a hotel, leaving Karinne and Max alone.

"You look like hell," Max said. "Can I fix you a drink?"

"No, thanks." She flopped down on the couch.

"Want to talk?" he asked, joining her.

"There's not much to say that you don't already know. Mom told Dad she wanted to take me with her. She was going to pretend we were both dead. You were right not to tell her where I was that day. Dad took the news pretty hard. I'm worried about him."

"He sounded calm when I talked to him on the phone," Max informed her.

"Thank heaven for that. Dad had divorce papers waiting. Mom walked in, he told her to sign them, and it went downhill from there. I stayed a while to talk to Dad, then came the drive home."

"Another emotional scene?"

"Yes. Mom asked me to go to Mexico."

"Why?"

"So I could have my lab work done in a country where Mom wouldn't worry about getting arrested. I refused."

"I imagine Margot wasn't pleased about that."

"She thought I was doing it for revenge." Karinne wrinkled her nose with disgust. "It's not that at all. I'm still willing to be tested, but I told her I was a last resort. She hasn't even bothered to put Jon on the donor list. And his father doesn't even know where they are. Jon should be *their* priority. Instead, she takes the easy way out—asks me. I guess that shows where I stand on her list."

"I think she really did want to see you, Karinne."

"For Jon."

"You're forgetting one thing. Margot could have avoided

trouble, avoided being charged with insurance fraud, by staying home. She took a risk coming here."

"Thank you for reminding me of that." Karinne willed herself not to cry. "I don't know what to believe anymore. But I *am* glad to know she's not dead. Glad she's had some happiness in her life. Thrilled to know I have a brother. I'll do the donor compatibility tests. But that's not going to change my plans. I'm quitting my job at the end of the month. After that, I'm moving up to the Grand Canyon. I'll find a new job somewhere—maybe with Flagstaff college sports."

Max took her in his arms. "You can't just walk away from your mother and brother."

"I think Mom's going to disappear again as soon as she can get two plane tickets."

"Then stop her," Max said. "You love your mother. Lord knows how long it'll be before you see her again. And Jon. Don't let her leave yet, Karinne. Ask her to stay."

She sat up straight on the couch, slipping out of his loving embrace. "This is a sudden change of heart."

He twisted a strand of her hair. "I've been wrong, too. One of the reasons I love you so much is your loyalty to your family. Despite Margot's treatment of you and your father, you care. And you offered to help a boy you've only known a few days. You're a strong woman, the kind of woman I admire. I can't disapprove of your actions when I want those same things, that same strength, for *our* family."

Karinne took a deep breath. "Are you willing to marry me?"

Max exhaled, gently touched her face, and laid her cheek against his chest. "Yes."

He kissed the top of her head and stroked her hair. "You should call your mother."

"No. In my life, you come first."

Their lovemaking chased away the harshness of the past and renewed their connection. They fell asleep in each other's arms. Only when Karinne woke later, refreshed in heart and soul, did she pick up the phone. The front desk of the hotel had a message for her.

"I'm sorry. Mrs. Lazar asked us to tell you that she'll wait to hear from you by phone regarding your donor status. She and her son have flown home to Mexico—she said they wanted to avoid any potential problems. Mrs. Lazar said you'd understand."

In other words, Margot had skipped bail and run away again. Max held Karinne in his arms again as she cried all the tears she'd held back as a child. After that she vowed she'd never cry over Margot again.

MAX DIDN'T LEAVE Karinne's side during the next few days, although she assured him she was fine.

"Don't you have to get back to work?" she asked him as she helped Anita pack up her belongings for the move north. Anita had found a job as an accountant at one of the banks just outside Grand Canyon Village. Cory had rented an apartment for them topside, and he was busy moving his things out of the place he and Max had shared for so long.

"We'll go back there together," Max said, "as soon as you're done with your business in Phoenix. I've hired a temporary worker to help Cory with the week's scheduled raft trips. I've also talked with Jeff, and we've met with my lawyer. We're going to see what he can do to have embezzlement charges against your mother dropped due to family hardship. At least that way she'd be able to travel back and forth from Mexico to Arizona to see you. Plus she'll need to show up in court for your father to get his divorce. And to attend our wedding, which, by the way, isn't going to be in November. We'll get married as soon as possible at the Grand Canyon. Margot will want to be there."

Privately, Karinne thought Margot would never be coming back, but she said, "Thank you, Max. Dad deserves some closure."

Max frowned, as if he knew what she was thinking, but he said nothing on that topic. "I've also made an appointment with a Realtor, like you asked."

Two days earlier, Jeff had finally admitted to Karinne that it was time to move. She recalled the conversation.... "I've been holding on to the house all these years because of the memories. Now..." He'd sighed shakily, and Karinne had realized how old her father had become. "I'm tired of rattling around in this big house. It was never the same after you left."

"Do you want to stay in Phoenix, Dad?" she asked.

"No. If you're going north with Max, I'd like to find a place there. Unless...unless you and Max would feel I'm crowding you."

"Dad, I could never feel that way! Nor Max, either."

Jeff's voice quavered slightly. "You should've married him years ago. I held you back, Karinne. I'm sorry."

Karinne grasped her father's hand, his arthritic fingers safely within her own. "I held myself back, Dad. You're not to blame."

"You always had a big heart, Karinne. Can you—" Jeff broke off.

"What, Dad?"

"Can you forgive your mother? She ran out on you—again."

"I know. But she left me a long time ago. And she can't do Jon any good if she's in jail, Dad."

"Hard to believe Margot has a son. And now Max is

trying to get the charges against her dropped on compassionate grounds."

"But I thought that was your idea, too!"

Jeff sighed again. "I'm ashamed to say it wasn't. It was generous of Max to say so, though. He's a better man than I am."

Karinne studied her father—the wrinkles on his face, the gray hair, the blue veins that stood out under the skin of his hands. She couldn't bear to see him so defeated.

"As a father, you have nothing to be ashamed of, Dad. I think Mom's disappearance was even worse for you than it was for me. I had you, Grandma and Max and Cory and their parents. You had no one except Grandma."

"Wrong, Karinne. I had you."

They both smiled, still hand in hand both letting go of the past and the bitterness. Jeff finally wiped his eyes.

"What comes next?" he asked.

"I get married," Karinne said simply.

"Is your mother coming? If you want her there, I'll be all right with it."

"I don't know what's going on with Margot. I haven't heard from her since she left. But I'm going to the hospital tomorrow to be tested as a possible donor. Max is driving me."

"Max told me what you said to Margot, that she should put Jon on the anonymous donor list first. If she finds a match there, I hope that isn't the last you hear from her. If you don't see her again, will you be okay?"

Karinne glanced around at her old home, childhood memories of Margot clinging to the familiar walls. Ghosts of the young Jeff and Margot and a little girl rose up, a happy family that had suddenly gone wrong.

"If she doesn't come back here, I'll go see her and Jon

in Mexico. She's my mother. I love her, Dad. I know she still loves me."

He nodded. "I have one thing to be grateful to Margot for—you."

"Now it's my turn to ask you, Dad. Are you going to be okay?"

"Of course I am," Jeff said brusquely. "I'm planning on dancing at your wedding and spoiling my grandchildren. You *are* going to give me grandchildren, aren't you?"

"It's definitely in the future." Karinne smiled. "To-morrow, Max and I are getting our blood tests for the wedding."

Max and Karinne went to the hospital lab the following day. In addition to the routine lab test required for marriage, Karinne's lab work included the donor compatibility test and a full scan. Margot had brought Jon's file to the transplant department before running south. Karinne was upset that her mother hadn't made time to say goodbye, but managed to drop off paperwork before her departure. She kept quiet about it. She stared at the bandage over her vein and wondered how Jon was doing. She'd had far too little time with him. But Max had bought Jon the promised cell phone and Karinne had the number. She planned to stay in touch.

"When will the results be in?" Karinne asked the lab tech.

"A few days." He threaded the labeled tubes of blood through the holes in the carrying tray. "There's a number you can call. They'll give it to you at the front desk."

"Thank you."

Max took her other arm. "Ready?"

"I am." Karinne pictured Margot and Jon. *I've done all I can.*

"Where now?" Max asked.

"I thought we could get something to eat, then I should go see my boss. I need to extend my medical coverage, do my exit interview, and say my goodbyes."

"Want me to come along?"

Karinne shook her head. "It won't take me long. But I'd like to go alone, if you don't mind."

"Of course not. You can drop me back at your apartment," he said.

KARINNE'S BOSS was regretful but resigned. "We're going to miss you, Karinne. I hate to see you give up a good career for marriage. It seems so...old-fashioned."

"I'm a photographer. I'm not giving that up," she said. "Just changing locations and settling down, that's all."

"Well, if you're sure..."

"I'm sure."

Her boss sighed. He rose from his desk to shake her hand. "Good luck. And you can always come back if living up north doesn't agree with you."

"Thanks." She shook his hand, then spontaneously hugged him. "I've enjoyed working here."

After a number of emotional farewells, she made her way outside to the parking lot and her car. She felt sad, but mostly she felt exhilarated, ready to face a new future. Perhaps she and Max should go out and celebrate tonight. Fresh starts should be marked like the milestones they were.

Her plan didn't happen. Max rose to meet her as soon as she walked in the door, his voice urgent. "You didn't answer your phone."

"I set it to voice mail when I went in to work. I guess I forgot to turn it back." She rummaged in her purse and pulled up her cell. "Yep, it's still on—"

"I think you'd better sit down," he said.

"Max? What's wrong?"

"Sit down," he repeated. She took a seat on the couch, and he sat beside her. "Remember when we first got engaged and you authorized me as your emergency contact?"

"Yes. What's up?"

"The hospital called. It's about your tests."

"Already?"

"The doctors want you to go back for more tests."

"Oh." She digested the news. "I guess I can do that. I'll go first thing tomorrow."

Max shook his head. "They want you to go there today, as an inpatient."

"What?"

"They think you have the same kidney disease your brother has, Karinne. Chronic kidney disease can run in families."

"I...I feel fine."

"You look fine. But so did Jon. I packed you an overnight bag. They're waiting for us."

Karinne swallowed hard. "You didn't tell Dad, did you?"

"No. But I did call Jon and asked him to tell your mother."

Transplant Surgical Ward,
Deserette Hospital, Flagstaff

A MONTH LATER, Max and Cory waited quietly outside the room while Karinne had one last pre-op exam by her doctors. Margot and Anita were in the room with her, the brothers outside with Jeff.

"I still can't believe Karinne needed the kidney transplant," Cory said, shaking his head. "Or that Margot would end up being her donor. If she hadn't come back..."

Max said nothing, but his face reflected the strain he'd been under ever since discovering the news.

"Good thing Jon's a candidate for that new treatment program," Cory said. "That and occasional dialysis will keep him out of surgery. And your work kept Margot out of jail. If you hadn't…"

Max nodded. His lawyer had been successful in getting the insurance company to drop charges on compassionate grounds. Shaken by the news of Karinne's illness, Jeff had helped with some of the transactions himself.

"She would've come back to Karinne even if the charges hadn't been dropped. And donating a kidney—I guess that makes up for some of the past. I just wish I'd been able to do more," Jeff said, for while Margot and Karinne were compatible tissue matches, Jeff and Karinne were not.

Jon and Karinne had not been donor matches, either, although one of Jon's cousins had shown both compatibility and a willingness to help if Jon needed it in the future. Karinne had the same progressive kidney disease as Jon did, moderate on the left side and heavily advanced and necrotic on the right. Unlike Jon, she hadn't responded to medication. Margot had immediately volunteered one of her own to replace Karinne's right kidney, which had to be removed. Today, she'd receive one of Margot's healthy organs.

Max and Karinne had talked last night, the night before the surgery. The couple had walked hand in hand to the hospital patio outside, the fierceness of the sun gone, the air flooded with desert moonlight.

"You okay about tomorrow? Not feeling guilty about taking Margot up on her offer?" Max had asked.

The doctors had told Karinne that a single healthy kidney could take over ninety-five percent of the function of a healthy pair. With only her one remaining kidney, she wouldn't be one-hundred-percent fit, but she wouldn't be an invalid, either. And she could still have children.

"I guess I'm still in shock about everything. It was one hell of a vacation, wasn't it? My mother comes back from the dead, I get a new brother, I end up in the hospital and Mom gets to play heroine, after all."

Max smiled. "Everyone else already had their turn, including you." Max had then told Karinne more about the events after she'd bravely left to go get the raft—Cory and Anita's strength, Jon's courage and, most of all, Margot's actions despite her despair.

"She never stopped looking for both you and Jon, Karinne. Cory said she kept those binoculars glued to her face during the whole time. She still had them when she went under. That's why she was trapped. Cory said the leather strap saved her...."

Karinne's lips parted. "He didn't tell me that."

"Without them, she would've been swept away. Cory wouldn't have found her." He paused. "Margot acted very selfishly, but it seems she never stopped loving you, Karinne."

Karinne had her own revelations. "She told me she came back to Arizona to see me during holidays, birthdays. To watch me from a distance... She even came to my graduation. I never guessed...I wish I'd known. And now...this. But Max, you don't seem surprised by my mother's about-face."

"Not now. I never would've believed she'd be your donor. Like your father, I was ready to write her off forever."

"Why didn't you?"

"Because you bring out the best in those around you, including me." Max pulled her closer. "You always have. It's a rare gift. You have a most positive effect on those around you. You're unselfish, so they are, too. Margot gives you a kidney. Jeff puts aside his rage and opens his home to Margot and Jon. Cory nearly drowns rescuing Margot. Jon went after you in a storm to prove himself a true member of your family...."

"Like you and Cory are," Karinne murmured.

"And even Anita goes on a rafting vacation with you, and the woman can't swim a stroke."

"I didn't know," Karinne said ruefully. "Besides, her husband was the main attraction, not me."

"She was your roommate and friend long before she married Cory." Max turned her in his arms. "You're a cut above the rest of us. I almost missed seeing that myself lately."

"Now, *that* I don't believe," Karinne said with a smile. "I made sure you noticed me as soon as I was out of school."

"I'm not talking about college days. I'm talking about this past week."

"I almost lost you. I thought I'd lost you all." Her voice cracked.

"But you didn't. In fact, you've gained something. I had a lot of time to think, floating in the water with Jon. I want children, Karinne. Our children. Adopted or biological. Whatever works out for us."

"Me, too. You'll make a good father, Max." The stars shone crisp and clear, but in Karinne's eyes they blurred for a moment. Beyond them, the desert night grew cooler. The owls and bats came out to soar and mate above the saguaros, while the coyotes howled to one another, like calling like. "Mom as a grandmother—now, that's a scary thought," Karinne said with a grin.

"I wouldn't worry."

"She and Jon are going back to Mexico after my surgery and the wedding—which is right after we check out of the hospital. No more rescheduling. I'm wishing for the fastest recovery on record."

"You'll both be all right," Max assured her. "By the way, Margot said she held nothing against me for lying to her all those years ago—because it would've been wrong to take you away from your home and Jeff."

"I'm glad." Karinne smiled. "I would never have had you if she had. Now kiss me."

And he did.

Chapter Nineteen

One year later,
Havasu Falls, Grand Canyon

The azure Arizona sky blazed above Havasu Falls as Max peeled off his shirt and tossed it over his backpack on the ground. A pair of golden eagles glided on the thermals above as he and Karinne shed the rest of their clothing to their swimsuits beneath. Max appreciatively took in Karinne's figure. The surgical scar had faded enough that she wore a two-piece suit instead of a maillot. Max thought her even more beautiful than before.

"And to think you wanted to spend our first anniversary in Hawaii," Karinne said as she unbuttoned her blouse.

Since their wedding at the Grand Canyon a year ago, Karinne had never wanted to leave, just as Max had always hoped. The magic of the canyon—or Max—had worked its spell on her. She and Margot had come through the surgery successfully. By the time both had recovered, Max and Jeff had arranged for the wedding to be outside at the rim of the canyon, at Karinne's insistence.

"Your home is my home now, Max. It's beautiful, more beautiful than any professional decor could be. I have my dress and veil—that's all I need. I don't want us to be apart again."

"But you've been planning a big church wedding for years," Max protested.

"Yes, I have, but I'm done with planning. Now all I want is to get married—at our new home."

Karinne got her wish.

With Anita and Cory as their witnesses, she and Max spoke their vows with the stunning colors of the Grand Canyon behind them. For Karinne, "family" now meant people she truly loved, not just blood kin. Cory and Max's mother was in that group. Like Max, they'd loved her since she was a child, while Anita had shown herself to be a true sister.

Jeff, Margot and Jon were also present. Afraid that Karinne and Max might elope, Jeff had agreed to Margot's presence, and was genuinely friendly to the young Jon.

Having the people she loved around her made her wedding complete, but it was Max who made *her* complete. He always had, and always would.

Now, emerald and turquoise water danced before them—the hot springs bubbling up from smooth, many-colored rocks. Hand in hand, they walked barefoot from pool to pool, the tiered levels gently stepping down in easy levels. Some levels lay above the main cascade. In the lower regions, a few teens swam in the deeper water, frolicking in the cascade's spray.

"What does *Havasupai* mean again?" Karinne asked.

"*Pai* is people, *Havasu* means blue-and-green waters. I told you earlier, remember?" Max asked.

"No. Next time you share any cultural facts, make sure I'm paying attention, okay?"

"I've tried," Max replied, "but you keep changing anthropology into anatomy lessons. My anatomy, to be specific. Not that I'm complaining, mind you..."

Karinne blushed. Romance in the great outdoors instead

of a bedroom was decadently new for her—and something she especially enjoyed. But then, much of her life was new. She'd left behind the old after Max had rescued her from the raft that July day when she'd seen Margot and fallen in. She'd emerged a different woman.

Karinne was exploring new horizons as a photographer. She'd assembled a portfolio of Colorado River and Grand Canyon shots. She now worked for the government, documenting geographic changes for river conservation efforts. Karinne had proudly become the latest photographer to carry on the photographic work started by Powell and his explorers. As long as the Colorado River continued to reshape the Grand Canyon, her future employment was ensured.

The waters of Havasu Falls, still Native American land smack in the middle of the canyon's national park, remained unchanged and pristine for their first anniversary. The prehistoric rocks parted deep below to give birth to hot springs. There, steaming water made its way up to the surface, heated by the earth's core. As the spring rose, it mingled with minerals from the deep crust. Instead of silt-colored red waters, or the clarity of clear, lake-bottom dam water, Havasu Creek bubbled up in waves of brilliantly colored blues and greens that danced and spilled over smooth curves of smooth boulders. The three rainbowed waterfalls gently scooped a network of tiered pools that led down to the Colorado.

"This is my favorite spot," Max said, taking her hand and leading her toward the Havasu waters.

"It's so beautiful."

Max drew Karinne into his lap, and they sat in waist-high water, his chin resting on her shoulder.

"What are you thinking?" Max asked, stroking away

wet hair from her forehead and tucking a strand behind her ear.

"Now that Jon's doing so well, he wants another vacation with us according to Mom. I guess that includes her, too."

"They were here just six weeks ago," Max said, a bit impatiently. "Your mother can't expect to make up for lost time all at once. We've only been married a year!"

They'd all come a long way since the flood more than a year ago. Following Karinne's example, Anita had decided to stay permanently in Grand Canyon Village. Both couples ended their long-distance relationships in favor of *much* closer proximity and planned for children in the future. Cory and Max argued over who'd be the most capable father. Max stoutly swore it would be him.

"I had you as a little brother to practice on," Max said.

"But I never showed you all my tricks," Cory told him. "So I'll be the better dad."

"I'll be around to help out—if you need me," Margot had volunteered. "Drop me a line or call. I'm only a short flight away."

Margot had also made some changes in her life. She told Stephan the whole truth about her past. It had taken him a while to get over the fact that Margot had lied to him about being a widow, and that she'd flown Jon to Arizona without his knowledge. Fortunately for Margot, Jeff was granted a speedy divorce.

Wisely, Margot had legally married Stephan in Mexico as soon as he calmed down. She made no mention of moving to Arizona, and remained content with her second family. However, she did convince Stephan that Jon should know his half sister, and allow them to visit.

Since then, Jeff had moved into a retirement village near the canyon. While he wasn't dating again, he'd made new friends, male and female. He'd even joined Karinne on some of her less-strenuous photographic sessions at the canyon.

"I guess Margot and Jon don't know the meaning of *newlywed,*" Max said.

"Don't forget Dad. He seems to enjoy popping up with his cameras whenever I have a trip planned."

"They just can't stay away from you."

"I think the great outdoors is the real draw," Karinne said modestly. "I can never get over how beautiful this is. The water is perfect and even Anita's enjoying it."

"At least she can swim now," Max added.

"I'm surprised she's not terrified of water.... I still can't believe how far she's come learning to be a river guide."

Karinne had seen Cory calmer and relaxed with Anita at his side. Anita and Cory would continue with the rafting business full-time. Max had offered them a half share, and they'd enthusiastically accepted. Anita was doing the books, too.

Yes, the "vacation from hell" had turned into something heavenly....

"Happy anniversary, Max." Karinne smiled.

"Same to you. But I didn't buy you a gift."

"That's okay. I have one for you." Karinne disengaged Max's hands from her waist. "It's in my pack."

Max climbed out of the water and pulled out a wrapped present. He unfolded the paper to reveal a boating catalog. One eyebrow raised in confusion, he carefully returned the wrapping and ribbon into her pack.

"I still owe you a boat engine, remember? I dropped yours at the pier during the monsoon."

"Karinne, don't be ridiculous. I'm not going to hold you accountable for that."

"But I'm determined to make amends." Karinne climbed

out of the water herself. "I've marked one I think you'll like. Check it out."

Max flipped to the folded catalog page. "These aren't engines or rafts. They're houseboats."

"That's right. By this time next year, we'll have to pack up the tents. I don't think your raft is big enough for a crib," she teased.

Max actually dropped the catalog. "The doctors...?"

"Gave me the green light. We can start trying for a baby anytime—tonight, if you want."

Max stared at her in wonder. Silently, they stood and left the waterfall hand in hand. Back on the private shores of the Colorado, they held each other close.

Sometime later, they lay, quietly satisfied, basking in the afterglow of a tender joining.

"So...like your present?" Karinne asked.

"Yeah, but I like the giver more than the gift. I do have to find a specialty dealer," Max murmured to himself. "Flagstaff's closer, although Phoenix might have more of a selection. What do you think?"

"I think I should've saved the catalog for tomorrow," she said with a laugh.

"You don't want to look?" he asked, one hand on his flashlight.

"Not now." Karinne yawned, rolling onto her side of the double sleeping bag. "If I wanted to read, I'd be nose-deep in the baby books I brought."

His reluctant bride had become a willing one, committed to their marriage and the baby to come.

He trusted her with his heart and his soul—because she *was* his heart and soul. Max let the beauty and magic of love flood his senses, thankful for the two of them, the desert stars and their triumph over the monsoon waters. He gathered her in his arms and held her close, knowing deep down inside that by saving Karinne from Margot all those years ago...

He'd saved her for himself.

* * * * *

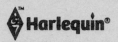

COMING NEXT MONTH

Available April 12, 2011

#1349 MY FAVORITE COWBOY
American Romance's Men of the West
Shelley Galloway

#1350 ONE WILD COWBOY
Texas Legacies: The McCabes
Cathy Gillen Thacker

#1351 A CONVENIENT PROPOSAL
Creature Comforts
Lynnette Kent

#1352 RODEO DADDY
Rodeo Rebels
Marin Thomas

REQUEST YOUR FREE BOOKS!
2 FREE NOVELS PLUS 2 FREE GIFTS!

 Harlequin®

 American ★ Romance®

LOVE, HOME & HAPPINESS

YES! Please send me 2 FREE Harlequin American Romance® novels and my 2 FREE gifts (gifts are worth about $10). After receiving them, if I don't wish to receive any more books, I can return the shipping statement marked "cancel." If I don't cancel, I will receive 4 brand-new novels every month and be billed just $4.24 per book in the U.S. or $4.99 per book in Canada. That's a saving of at least 15% off the cover price! It's quite a bargain! Shipping and handling is just 50¢ per book in the U.S. and 75¢ per book in Canada.* I understand that accepting the 2 free books and gifts places me under no obligation to buy anything. I can always return a shipment and cancel at any time. Even if I never buy another book, the two free books and gifts are mine to keep forever.

154/354 HDN FDKS

Name	(PLEASE PRINT)

Address	Apt. #

City	State/Prov.	Zip/Postal Code

Signature (if under 18, a parent or guardian must sign)

Mail to the **Reader Service:**
IN U.S.A.: P.O. Box 1867, Buffalo, NY 14240-1867
IN CANADA: P.O. Box 609, Fort Erie, Ontario L2A 5X3

Not valid for current subscribers to Harlequin American Romance books.

Want to try two free books from another line?
Call 1-800-873-8635 or visit www.ReaderService.com.

* Terms and prices subject to change without notice. Prices do not include applicable taxes. Sales tax applicable in N.Y. Canadian residents will be charged applicable taxes. Offer not valid in Quebec. This offer is limited to one order per household. All orders subject to credit approval. Credit or debit balances in a customer's account(s) may be offset by any other outstanding balance owed by or to the customer. Please allow 4 to 6 weeks for delivery. Offer available while quantities last.

Your Privacy—The Reader Service is committed to protecting your privacy. Our Privacy Policy is available online at www.ReaderService.com or upon request from the Reader Service.

We make a portion of our mailing list available to reputable third parties that offer products we believe may interest you. If you prefer that we not exchange your name with third parties, or if you wish to clarify or modify your communication preferences, please visit us at www.ReaderService.com/consumerchoice or write to us at Reader Service Preference Service, P.O. Box 9062, Buffalo, NY 14269. Include your complete name and address.

HARI I

Selene wanted nothing to do with the father of her son, Alex; but Aristedes had other plans...that included them.

Read on for an sneak peek from
THE SARANTOS SECRET BABY by Olivia Gates,
available April 2011, only from Harlequin Desire.

"You were right to turn my marriage offer down," Aristedes said.

And Selene found her voice at last, found the words that would not betray the blow he'd dealt her. "Thanks for letting me know. You didn't have to come all the way here, though. You could have just let it go. I left yesterday with the understanding that this case is closed."

Before the hot needles behind her eyes could dissolve into an unforgivable display of stupidity and weakness, she began to close the door.

The door stopped against an immovable object. His flat palm.

"I can't accept that." His voice was low, leashed.

What did her tormentor mean now? Was he ending one game only to start another?

She raised eyes as bruised as her self-respect to his, found nothing there but solemnity and determination.

Before she could voice her confusion, he elaborated. "I never let anything go unless I'm certain it's unworkable. I realize I made you an unworkable offer, and that's why I'm withdrawing it. I'm here to offer something else. A workability study."

She leaned against the door, thankful for its support and partial shield. "Your son and I are not a business venture you can test for feasibility."

His gaze grew deeper, made her feel as if he was trying to delve into her mind, take control of it. "It's actually the

SDEXP0411

other way around. I'm the one who would be tested."

She shook her head. "Why bother? I know—and *you* know—you're not workable. Not with me."

His spectacular eyebrows lowered over eyes she felt were emitting silver hypnosis. "You're right again. Neither you nor I have any reason to believe that isn't the truth. The only truth. It might be best for both you and Alex to never hear from me again, to forget I exist. But then again, maybe not. I'm only asking for the chance for both of us to find out for certain. You believe I'm unworkable in any personal relationship. I've lived my life based on that belief about myself. I never really had reason to question it. But I have one now. In fact, I have two."

Find out what happens in
THE SARANTOS SECRET BABY by Olivia Gates,
available April 2011, only from Harlequin Desire.

Copyright © 2011 by Olivia Gates

SDEXP0411

MARGARET WAY

In the Australian Billionaire's Arms

Handsome billionaire David Wainwright isn't about to let his favorite uncle be taken for all he's worth by mysterious and undeniably attractive florist Sonya Erickson.

But David soon discovers that Sonya's no greedy gold digger. And as sparks sizzle between them, will the rugged Australian embrace the secrets of her past so they can have a chance at a future together?

Don't miss this incredible new tale,
available in April 2011
wherever books are sold!

www.eHarlequin.com

HR17722